Uranium Downs

Jessica Bertrand

BROKEN YOKE
PUBLISHING

Uranium Downs

Published by Broken Yoke Publishing, LLC.
BrokenYokePublishing.com

ISBN: 978-1-955941-03-7

Dedication

To you. Because it’s time to discover the hero in you.

Reader’s Note

Tressa Lykios is deaf, she communicates using American Sign Language (ASL). ASL doesn’t use articles like a, an, the, of, etc. so expect the sentences to be a little different. You’ll see the ASL dialogue in all caps throughout the story. Have fun!

Chapter 1

"Do we have to, Mrs. McCreedy?" Cora's voice, aka Miss Perfect, grated like nails across a chalkboard, setting my nerves on edge. Her curly brown hair bounced when she flicked it over her shoulder with flawless nails. I'm so glad I didn't have to grow up with her. Were all sophomores this annoying? Was I?

Monica Estes, my library friend, scrunched her nose and crossed her eyes at me, I bit my lip to keep from laughing out loud. Monica, in cute Manga mode, wore her black hair straight with her bangs cut across the top of her eyebrows. Her white button-up shirt tucked into a skirt that barely made it to her knees. Knee-length socks disappeared into her black Converse sneakers that were showing their wear and tear around the edges.

"You don't have to," Mrs. McCreedy glided toward the first row of desks. Her green, tartan-patterned dress swished against her legs. A stark contrast to her fiery red hair. If it wasn't in a bun, would she look like the girl off of *Brave*?

"You could simply fail my history class for the quarter."

"What?" Miss Perfect put her hand to her chest. "Since when's this project graded? My sister said it wasn't last year."

"I also didn't teach at Orchard Mesa High School last year." Mrs. McCreedy raised both of her eyebrows.

I snorted and clamped a hand over my mouth. Miss Perfect narrowed her eyes at me.

Mrs. McCreedy focused on the clock. "Since we only have five or six minutes remaining in the period, I want you to get into groups for the history project. This will go to competition."

The noise level cranked up when everyone moved tables and chairs around to get into groups. I turned to my left, the new girl sat at the last desk in the front row. Her American Sign Language (ASL) interpreter gave her a half-hearted grin. Making friends ended up difficult to begin with, but what if others feared reaching out to her?

Before I knew it, I stood in front of her desk. I signed, HI. MY NAME A-M-I-E C-O-L-E-M-A-N.

MY NAME T-R-E-S-S-A L-Y-K-I-O-S. Her dark eyes sparkled, and a smile spread across her tanned face. A pink ribbon held her black hair back in a smooth ponytail. She wore a light pink blouse with olive drab capris and pink flats.

NICE MEET YOU. I responded.

HOW YOU KNOW ASL? Tressa tilted her head.

MY AUNT. My eyes misted, and I swallowed. Tressa waited. DIED LAST YEAR.

Tressa stuck out her lip and rolled a fist in a circle on her chest. SORRY.

SAME. I added, YOU, ME. GROUP TOGETHER? Moving my fist around like I stirred a pot.

Tressa's face brightened. YES. MORE PEOPLE TOGETHER? YOU FIND.

OKAY. YOU WANT COME? I took a step away.

Tressa glanced around. The buzz of voices made my head swim. She shook her head no and motioned for me to go. Auntie taught me how many people don't understand the deaf and are hostile or uncomfortable around them. It takes courage for them to live everyday with people thinking they ignore them only because they can't hear.

Monica talked with a couple of other girls I recognized from the Manga Club, who met in the library to discuss their favorite books and movies. She waved me over. "Amie, we almost got our group figured out. We only need one more. Don't worry, you'll fit right in."

"Oh. Only one more spot?" I wrinkled my nose.

"What'd you do?" Monica's shoulders drooped. I half expected her to morph into a cartoon with Manga-sized tear drops to shower me.

"The new girl, Tressa, needed to be in a group. She joined mine. I came to ask you all the same question." I winced. Would she still be my friend after this?

"The deaf girl? Who'd want her in any group?" Pierce Estes walked by us glaring at Tressa. His dark hair had a white skunk stripe down the middle and he dressed all in black.

The color drained out of Monica's face. Having an idiot for a cousin wasn't her fault.

"Don't you have someone to go tackle?" My jaw clenched. I tightened my fist into a ball. My horrible comebacks needed work.

"Maybe, *if* I played football. I skateboard." Pierce rolled his eyes and ambled away from us giving the side of his skinny jeans a hitch. His narrow hips made the adjustment pointless. Pierce angled around the cool girls and shoulder checked a tall kid in nice jeans and a light brown button-down shirt. Tall Kid glared at Pierce but turned and sat down in his seat, engrossed in his phone. I know he was newer, but not as new as Tressa.

"Sorry," Monica squeaked. "Pierce is *so* not joining our group."

"Ditto." I agreed.

The silence hung awkward between us. Monica's three friends switched their gazes between the two of us.

"Uh. I guess we're competing with each other instead of being on the same team." My shoe scuffed the floor.

"Looks that way." Monica countered.

"I hope we both make it to the next round." I smiled.

"See you in the library tomorrow?" Worry creased Monica's forehead.

"Count on it." She hugged me, her sigh audible. Friendship doesn't need sound. After releasing Monica I returned to sit next to Tressa again.

WOW. Tressa must've lip read what Pierce said because she pointed at him, and her next sign made my jaw drop. Tressa smirked and her interpreter raised a warning eyebrow.

"Can I join your group?" The school's computer genius, Josh Zovko, had us all looking up. He spiked his blond hair today, and his dirt brown t-shirt hung loose on his lanky frame.

Tressa finished watching her interpreter sign. I shrugged at Tressa when she looked at me. She returned the gesture in a sure-why-not sort of way.

"Even if I can't talk with my hands?" Josh held out his hands as if he didn't know what to do with them.

HE WORRY, DON'T SIGN. I pointed at Josh.

Tressa waved it away. Josh took out his phone, texted something on the screen and sat next to her, showing what he wrote. She slapped his arm, opened an app, and started off a fast-paced texting battle. They shoved screens into the other's face before their thumbs went back to typing.

Scanning the room, I found almost everyone who wanted to be in groups were congregating. Some stood at Mrs. McCreedy's desk signing up for individual projects or papers. Monica's team looked determined. Pierce mingled with the other skaters, and the wrestling team cracked jokes.

Tall Kid and Josh had the same build. As if in sync with each other, they both shifted and placed an ankle on their knees. Hmm. Tall Kid used his left hand to take a drink of water. Josh favored his left hand too, yet I'd never seen either of them acknowledge the other. Maybe it'd been a freak occurrence.

Tressa made a small attention-grabbing wave, she'd caught me staring at the new guy. She pointed at Tall Kid then me finishing with the sign for sweethearts.

NO SWEETHEART. ONLY ME. I rolled my eyes.

The look on Tressa's face said she didn't believe me. ASK JOIN. NEXT. SWEETHEARTS. She batted her lashes.

Heat crept up my neck.

Tressa laughed.

Josh looked up from writing the next part of their conversation. "Did I miss something?"

Tall Kid, oblivious to the clamor of voices surrounding him, didn't even flinch when a wad of paper from the back of the room bounced off the side of his head. I moved to stand in front of his desk.

"If you want to run solo for the history project, you'll have to tell Mrs. McCreedy now." Tall Kid didn't even acknowledge me. Maybe he didn't hear? I turned to look back at Tressa and shrugged. Josh's confused face ricocheted between the two of us. Tressa motioned for me to hit Tall Kid upside the head.

REALLY? I frowned.

Tressa kissed the air and wiggled her eyebrows. If I wasn't going to hit him, why would I kiss him?

GROSS. Swiveling, I found myself staring into Tall Kid's angry hazel eyes, which reflected the brown from his shirt. His dark hair was slicked back

"What do you want?" He sounded annoyed.

"Mrs. McCreedy said anyone who is going solo on a project needs to let her know." I blame Tressa for getting me flustered.

"Whatever." He stood, lifted his backpack to his shoulder, and started toward the door.

"I came over to ask if you wanted to be in our group."

Tall Kid paused. He looked at me, then Tressa, and Josh. Tressa gave him a little wave, but a Cheshire Cat grin plastered itself across her face. This was going to be a long project.

His sigh came out closer to a growl, “Sure, why not.”

“See ya next class.” Did I just add Pierce’s moody double to our group? I nodded to Tressa. She held up four fingers, our group total.

“You’re the boss.”

Chapter 2

Walking home from school meant the street didn't always have a sidewalk, but most of the time it had a bicycle lane. It was a great day to go biking, if I had friends to go with me. The River Front Trail went all the way to Fruita from behind the middle school. All the locals love to meander down it, even if it's miles long. Maybe Tressa and Monica would go with me. It'd make for a fun Saturday activity.

I kicked a pinecone out of my way. It skittered into the street crunching under the wheels of a passing car. When will Dad and Mom come back from Australia or Africa? What started out as an African safari turned into a volunteer effort to stop a wildfire in Australia. Living with Grandpa during the fire season was normal for me. Dad's wildland firefighting hotshot crew got called out and Mom went to work dispatch. We talked about moving a lot, but since Grandpa wasn't getting any younger, neither wanted to be too far away. Grandpa took care of me, but sometimes I think I babysat him instead when it came to entertainment. He said I kept him young.

The houses in my neighborhood seemed similar, but it all depended on when they were built. Several tri-level houses graced the street, but some — like mine — were two story homes. My cellphone read 4:10 pm, which meant I'd find Grandpa cooking supper. Grandma had diabetes so Grandpa made sure they ate early. He never changed that after she died. I skipped up the steps leading into the house and turned left at the front door of the small, enclosed porch.

"I'm home." The screen slammed behind me and I closed the door.

"In here." The scent of cookies wrapped me in a warm hug. I followed my nose to the kitchen. Washing my hands, I crept over and spooned some of the chocolate chip dough into my hand.

Grandpa straightened from beside the lower oven and closed the door. He put the latest tray of steaming cookies on a potholder before transferring them to a cooling rack. "Stay outta my cookie dough, Scamp."

"I don't know what you're talking about." My words muffled together, caught with a mouth full of sweet deliciousness.

"Uh-huh." The look he gave me said he didn't believe me for a minute. Grandpa looped his arm around my neck, I was stuck next to his ribcage. He kissed the top of my head and I pulled myself out from the circle his arm made. My hair poofed out electrified. Touching his bare elbow with my finger discharged the staticky build up. Grandpa jumped and poked the tickle spot on my ribcage.

Squealing, I made a hasty exit up the small flight of stairs to my bedroom and dropped my school stuff there. Switching to a shirt I could get cookie dough all over, because you never knew what might happen in the kitchen. I tiptoed downstairs with dough stealing on my mind. Poking my nose around the corner, I found Grandpa setting a few dishes in the sink. My hand settled on the counter, Grandpa turned and gave me an appraising look.

"We were assigned a group project today in history." Diversionary tactics.

"That's not good," he frowned. "The last project you ended up being stuck with all of the work."

"I'll make sure to delegate better this time." I sidled up to him.

"Sure you will." Grandpa gave me his best yeah-right look and snatched the bowl out of reach. He bumped my hip.

"Besides, I don't even know if I'm the group leader."

"Amie," Grandpa put the last of the cookie dough on the sheet and put it in the top oven. He'd remodeled the kitchen last year and added in a double stacked oven. "Your organizational skills and your excitement to learn usually put you among the top slots for grade earners in your classes."

I sighed. Mom and Dad did teach me a lot about being prepared. Grandpa handed me the mixing bowl and pointed toward the sink. The last ball of dough rested on the bottom. It disappeared into my mouth.

"Who's in your group?" Grandpa waited for me to finish chewing.

"The tall kid who started a couple of weeks ago, our favorite computer genius–Josh, and Tressa. She started today, and she's deaf."

"What about Monica? Aren't you two attached at the hip?"

"She already had four in her group and Tressa needed someone."

"That'd do it. Invite Tressa over." Grandpa shook his hand. "It's about time I dusted the arthritis off my joints."

Grandpa pointed to the fridge, "Since you're startin' supper with dessert, you need to end it with salad. Can you start preppin' the extras?"

I gasped. No more cookies?

Grandpa leaned his head back and laughed. "Wait 'til they're finished cookin'." He shook his head. "What are you researching?"

"I dunno." I pulled out the carrots, celery, bell pepper, and cucumber and started fixing the salad. "We're talking about it tomorrow."

"Any ideas?"

"I was thinking about the Uranium Boom. Will you help?" My best begging smile slid across my face.

"Help with the boom? I already did that."

"Grandpa," my growling only made him laugh.

The doorbell rang.

"I'll do what I can." He gave me a side hug. I pulled his wallet out of his pocket and headed to the door. Tonight was pizza night.

Chapter 3

Undisclosed Location in Town

"Skunk, I can't believe you. All of this training. All of this planning and you almost blew it." She paced back and forth, her heels clicking across the ceramic kitchen tiles. He sneered, hating the nickname.

"But I didn't." He crossed his hands over his chest, heart beating a defiant staccato.

She went nose to nose with him. "You have to win her trust. We can't afford to fail in retrieving it."

Same story, different state, different school.

He wiped her spittle from his cheek. "Trust takes time. Nothing failed."

"You've had time, lots of it."

He rolled his eyes, "Everything's fine."

She slapped him. It wasn't the first time, and probably not the last. Heat slid from his face to his gut where it formed a rock. Jaw clenched, he glared at her.

“Don’t sass me,” she hissed. “Just get it done.”

Chapter 4

Amie

Pierce came into the library and plopped down into one of the armchairs scattered around the space. His right cheek looked puffy. He skulked or pouted, I wasn't sure which one, but giving him a wide berth was goal number one.

Monica and I spent an hour in the library after lunch as student workers. She'd arrive in a few minutes. I grabbed the books needing shelved and wheeled the cart out to the stacks. Humming a catchy tune that Grandpa whistled before I left for school, I started sliding the returned items into place.

"Hey." I pivoted to find Pierce behind me. I was trapped. No way out unless I vaulted the book cart. My grip tightened a little around one of the hard-covered books in my hand, uncertainty trickled down my spine.

"What happened to your face?" Sarcasm dripped from my mouth.

"Nothin'." Pierce jutted his jaw out. "What happened to yours?"

"D'you need help finding a book?" I squeaked. Great comeback.

"Nah. Who needs books?" He pushed a book further into the shelf.

"Everyone." I tried to keep the frustration out of my voice without much success.

"Beside the point. My mom said I should apologize for being rude yesterday."

"Your mom's demanding an apology?" I cocked my head, he's not sorry. "It's Tressa who you need to talk to."

"Maybe another time." He shrugged. "Can I be in your group?"

"Nope." I slammed the book on the shelf, white-knuckle gripped the cart, and pushed it further up the aisle.

"Ah. Come on. Why not?" My new shadow refused to leave.

"Because you're not a good fit for the group. And I'd have to ask the others."

"So it's a maybe?" A sly smile spread over his face.

"No. It's a no."

"What do the others say?" Pierce trailed me out the end and I flipped the cart between us.

"We say no." Tall Kid came out from a different row and planted himself in a wide stance next to the cart, crossing his arms over his chest which made his shoulders broader. He wore a shirt with a bicycle racing logo on it. I swallowed, glad he was on my side.

Pierce huffed and walked away.

"Thanks, Tall Kid." Did I call him that? The heat from my face traveled to my toes. Ducking my head, I yanked the cart and jabbed the next book on the shelf.

"It's Drake." His voice was flat.

Clearing my throat, I turned to him. "Drake, right."

He narrowed his gaze at me, shook his head, and walked away.

Chapter 5

Monica pulled her Pokémon sweater on and collected her backpack. “Pierce is so annoying. What just happened?”

“He was apologizing.” I added in air quotes.

Monica hit the library exit door with a clang and we merged into the class change bedlam. She snorted, “Ha. That’ll be the day. He’s up to something.”

“It didn’t feel like an apology.”

“We need to keep an eye on him.”

I dodged a kid and bounced my elbow off a locker. “Ouch. He also asked about joining my group.”

“Figures. What’d you say?” Monica shook her head.

“No.”

“Good. Did it stick?” She knows her cousin.

“Nope. But Drake stopped by and reaffirmed it.”

“Drake?” Monica’s brow knotted.

“Tall Kid.” My ears started to burn, I called him that again. At least he wasn’t here to hear it.

"No way. That guy never comes to the library. What'd he want?"

"A book." We rounded the corner and came to Mrs. McCreedy's door. I took a drink from my water bottle.

"I thought he was allergic to books or something."

I choked on the water. Several students avoided the library like it was the plague. A little learning never hurt anyone.

"Amie," Mrs. McCreedy studied me for a minute.

"Yes, Ma'am." I croaked.

"Are you alright?"

I nodded.

"Good, please sit with your group without moving desks yet."

Josh already sat next to Tressa. I found a place at the desk behind her since she was at the front. Tressa turned, her eyes sparkling. Her hair was in a bun today.

I put both of my fists together near my heart and moved my thumbs. SWEETHEARTS?

I WISH. She stole a dreamy glance in Josh's direction, but he didn't notice it.

MY GRANDPA WANTS YOU COME DINNER MY HOUSE.

Tressa did a happy dance in her chair. WHEN?

I DON'T KNOW.

SOON?

I HOPE. HE WANT KNOW YOUR FAVORITE FOOD.

D-O-L-M-A.

WHAT THAT? I cocked my head.

GRAPE LEAVES.

LIKE K-A-L-E? I wrinkled my nose.

NO. She snapped her index and middle finger together with her thumb. G-R-E-E-K.

LIKE SALAD.

Tressa shook her head and launched into the fastest explanation of how to make them I'd ever seen.

"What did you say?" Josh whispered, staring wide-eyed at all the motions.

"Nothing." I hadn't taken my eyes of off Tressa, counting on my peripheral vision being accurate. "She's teaching me how to cook something.

Tressa ended by snatching her phone from her backpack. She showed me a picture. I'd seen them at the grocery store once or twice. They look like fried spring rolls, only green and a lot smaller in size.

OH. I SEE. GREEN SPRING ROLL. I snickered.

She groaned with exasperation and put her head on the back of her chair. Catching my smirk, she signed, FUNNY YOU.

Pointing at my nose, I put on my most innocent face. When I relaxed it, I added, WHERE I BUY?

NO. I MAKE.

OK. WHAT YOU NEED?

Tressa hesitated. MY GRANDMA MAKE WITH LAMB. BUT EXPENSIVE.

I ASK GRANDPA.

WANT FRESH GRAPE LEAF, BUT IN JAR OK.

MY FRIEND HAVE GRAPE VINE, I WILL SEE.

Tressa thumped the table. It was loud enough for the wrestlers to quiet down. She stood and gave me a big hug. I couldn't breathe for three seconds.

I FORGET. TEXT ME LIST PLEASE.

YES. THANK YOU.

I tapped my wrist and signed class.

Tressa bounced into her chair and focused on her interpreter.

Drake slipped into the empty seat next to me. Mrs. McCreedy looked at the clock and them him. He held up a hand in a silent wave accentuated by a sheepish grin.

Mrs. McCreedy explained the different types of projects we could do as well as what each would require. "Now it's time to get into your groups and decide what you'll research and how you will present that research to the judges. The competition will take place with other schools in our gym the Saturday before Christmas break." Moans floated through the room. "Your parents are already aware of this. Don't forget your topic has to fit the theme. Okay, get to work."

Tressa rocketed to her feet and motioned Josh to move. She grabbed her chair out of the way and brought her hands together. We all pushed our desks toward each other. Tressa guided her interpreter to a spot next to Drake and sat across from her.

IT OK I HAVE, I pointed to the interpreter. SIGN? Talking and signing at the same time didn't come easy.

K-A-T-H-L-E-E-N, the interpreter signed.

THANKS, I grinned at Kathleen. She nodded in response.

TIME START. Tressa bounced in her chair.

"If someone else wants to lead, I'm fine with it. But I have a couple of ideas on where to start."

Drake shrugged.

"What do you have?" Josh leaned his elbows on the desk.

"I cut some half sheets of paper and thought we'd write down our favorite things or what we want to learn about."

The constant buzz of students planning or talking in groups around the room, faded into the background while we wrote ideas to research down on the paper. Tressa slid hers to the middle of the table first: Greek mythology, service dogs, hearing aids, foster care, Greek heroes. Josh's list: mountain biking, ancient computers, high tech gear, mountain climbing, Bosnia and Kosovo history, World War I. Drake's: BMX, hiking, baseball, mining, gold rush.

Mine: Bookbinding, libraries, uranium mining, deaf studies.

"BMX." Josh made a face.

"What's wrong with it?" Drake's back snapped straight and his eyes narrowed.

"Uh guys." Neither paid attention to my warning.

"Everything. The way people ride them kills their knees. It's a ridiculous sport." Josh planted his hands on the desk and angled forward.

A vein popped in Drake's neck, his face reddened, and his body posture mirrored Josh's, "And mountain biking isn't."

Tressa's head bobbed between the two, enthralled at the excitement. Josh and Drake were now nose to nose with each other, obscuring Kathleen from view.

"Have you ever been to a BMX race?" Drake ground out through gritted teeth.

"I'd rather eat worms."

My mind went blank. How could I stop them? Maybe if I distracted them with something, they'd refocus. What did I have?

Knitting!

It was soft and if I tossed it right, the needles wouldn't poke either of them. Reaching into my backpack, I brought out the sky blue pouch I kept it in and gave it an overhand toss. That felt a little heavier than normal.

Oh no! I had a library book in there. One of the hardcovered ones.

Time slowed down. I had a great aim. The knitting pouch hiding the book swiveled end over end and hit both boys flat on the sides of their faces.

My cold hands covered my mouth, cheeks flaming. Their heads rotated toward me, their expressions dark.

Chapter 6

"And that's how I ended up with after school detention and two days of in school suspension next week. Technically they don't do after school detention, but because parent-teacher conferences are tonight, I get to go home when you're finished talking with teachers." My voice quivered, this was new territory for me, first time calling home because I was in trouble at school. When calling home from the office, the school phone became mandatory, "Grandpa? Hello?"

Did we get disconnected? Pressing my ear to the receiver and I heard a strangled gasp on the other end. No heart failure here, I should've recognized it earlier. "Don't forget to breathe."

"Is your Grandpa okay, Dear?" The secretary's southern drawl was as sweet as honey.

"Yes, Ma'am. He'll be fine once he catches his breath."

"Is it the shock and horror of you being in trouble? You're not one of the regulars, even I'm mortified Amie."

I ducked my head, the knot in my gut twisted. "No Ma'am. He's laughing."

Her jaw dropped, "Well, I never…"

Hanging up the phone, I slunk to the chair next to Tressa. Kathleen already talked with Tressa's mom. Josh went over to call his mom. Tressa stole a glance at me and then straightened her head. She snorted and started laughing too.

NOT THAT FUNNY, I told her.

I guess there was a first time for everything. Why it had to be me, I don't know. If the book had hit at a different angle, it could've sent one, or both, of the boys to the hospital. If they'd moved, the knitting pouchbook projectile would've hit Kathleen. It could've broken her nose. Not the brightest idea I've ever had.

Mom and Dad scheduled a video chat later tonight. I cringed. How much trouble would I be in then?

Mr. Beemer, the assistant principal, emerged to the waiting area. He motioned us to follow him and he led us up the hallway. The bell rang and a wall of students streamed through the halls. We waltzed our way through the curious glances of onlookers, some snickered. I turned away.

My steps slowed and my chest tightened. The assistant principal angled toward the library entrance. We were walking into my space. My home away from home.

Might as well hang a billboard sized advertisement that read, "Look here." Add a neon sign around my neck and we'd be solid. Too bad the school didn't have a dungeon. For one it'd be cooler and two, no one would know I was there. I could live on bread and water, no problem. No friends seeing me or witnessing my downfall.

What a horrible new experience.

Of course, Monica and the Manga Club gathered in the library today for an after school meeting.

I marched in, eyes forward, head held high. The lump in my stomach turned into molten lead. Monica winced, her face mirrored the horror rolling around my chest.

Shame heated my cheeks. I slid into a chair in the class meeting and instruction area. The start of detention in the library. The backs of my eyes burned, my brain and body couldn't decide. Would it be better to puke or cry? My eyes drilled holes into the varnished tabletop. I heard the others bump something on the tables when they sat.

"Ah. The perfect one gets in trouble at last." Pierce murmured and slithered into a seat at a table near me. "How's it feel good girl?" He over-emphasized the last part.

"Shove it, skunk face." Josh responded. I looked up and frowned.

"What'd you call me?" Pierce hissed, standing at the challenge. Mr. Beemer set some papers on the circulation counter.

Uh. Oh.

AGAIN. Tressa signed. She scooted forward in her chair, waiting for the next thing to happen. This was fast becoming her sport to watch.

Josh moved an eyebrow, but he seemed to be looking past Pierce, not at him. I turned to follow Josh's gaze. Drake caught the leg of my chair and plowed into Pierce, who landed on the floor.

"Sorry about that." Drake gripped Pierce's elbow and hauled him upright. He plopped Pierce into his chair and patted his shoulder. "Amie's chair was sticking out too far."

My brow knotted, and tears pooled in the corners of my eyes. Drake bent next to my chair and retrieved the backpack he'd dropped. I almost missed the wink when he straightened to his full height, plopped into his own designated space, and shared a nod with Josh. Mr. Beemer returned and scrutinized the boys.

Never before had the solitude of being an only child bothered me. I had plenty of practice with self-entertaining and alone time. I didn't have siblings to fight with. Was that my trouble? Were we going to end up as a family squabbling every time we had to make a decision?

Would Grandpa hand me my punishment or would he leave it to my parental unit? I pulled the scraps of paper we fought over out of my pocket. Mr. Beemer looked over my shoulder when I crossed off the BMX and mountain bike ideas. He circulated through the other tables. “Homework is a good idea.”

STUDY, I signed to Tressa.

I took off two of my other ideas. No one seemed keen on reading. This was going to be a long project. There weren’t any other repeats except for mining. Flipping over my paper I re-wrote the list into one big one.

How were we ever going to be a team? Would Josh and Drake get through their hatred over a different kind of bike sport? They’d communicated earlier, or was that a fluke? Could we agree on a topic?

Pierce’s head dipped to his chest and he shook it trying to stay awake. Josh was reading a manual on the 3-D printer in the Tech Ed class. Drake rubbed the side of his face, his cheek puffy from where the book hit it. He frowned at me. I shifted back to what I was working on. My stomach rolled. His swelling was my fault.

Mr. Beemer’s walkie talkie crackled to life, “Parents are here and ready to take their kids.”

Chapter 7

I found Grandpa outside of the school office, waiting with most of the other parents once set free from the library. Arms crossed over his barrel chest, he smiled at me. People always ask him if he lifted weights. He still had most of his hair, even though ninety percent of it was white. Grandpa chuckled and shook his head. Would he laugh all the way home too?

NEW GIRL? Grandpa signed and pointed to Tressa. FORGOT NAME.

Tressa dashed to him and wrapped her arms around Grandpa. Surprise flashed through his eyes, he forgot how the deaf hug when they get connected through sign language. He smiled and patted her head.

Tressa's mom dressed in sweatpants and a t-shirt. Her hunched shoulders and dark bags under her eyes screamed exhaustion. She pulled at Tressa's arm and they exited the building.

We followed close behind. Pierce slammed the passenger door of an SUV and it peeled out of the parking lot. Josh walked out to his Jeep, got in, and trailed his Mom's minivan toward the school's exit. Drake's dad was a little shorter than his son. They both had dark hair. I caught part of their conversation when they passed by us.

"You have to watch that angry streak in you, Son. You can't fight everyone who says something bad about BMX racing," his Dad scolded.

Drake hung his head. His ears turned pink.

"See you tomorrow, Drake." I waved.

"We'll pick up fighting over topics again." He rubbed the back of his neck.

"Sorry about hitting you with the book."

Drake shrugged it off.

His dad stopped, "Who's this?"

"The leader of our group in history," a storm brewed across Drake's face.

Grandpa made the introductions and they shook hands.

"New friends are always good," Drake's dad's smile didn't reach his eyes. "You can see friends tomorrow. Mom's in a late meeting, we're getting dinner."

Everyone turned when Josh's Jeep reversed over the speed bump and pulled to a stop next to me.

"Show off. Next time turn around first." I groused at him.

Josh gave me a cheeky grin, "It's more fun this way."

"Why aren't you going home?" Josh ignored my snarkiness.

"Grandpa has a flat tire. I didn't see it until I was almost out of the parking lot. Mom gave me permission to help change it." He closed the Jeep door and strode over to the 1950s era truck. Josh's dad helped find a couple of the parts to restore the collectable last summer.

Grandpa inspected his front tire and scratch the stubble on his cheek. "Hmm. So it is."

Drake examined it too.

Josh and Drake had a future in a NASCAR pit crew someday. Between them they exchanged tires in a little over six minutes. Beaming they high fived each other with greasy hands.

"Thank you, gentlemen." Grandpa opened his door.

"Nice hat, Grandpa," Josh swiped the hard hat off the seat and put it on. "It even comes with a headlamp."

Light blinded me when Josh swept the beam around the group.

"Yup. It was my old mining hat." Grandpa shielded his eyes.

"What'd you mine?" Drake dropped the flat tire in the truck bed with a loud clang and leaned his forearms on the side.

Grandpa knocked on the side of his hard hat, "Coal. Uranium. I tried gold once. Only ended up finding a cold."

We all laughed.

Josh set the hat back on the seat. "Amie, mining was one of your categories, right?"

I nodded.

"We could do that for our project." Josh pointed at Grandpa, "We'd have access to a real miner and add his stories in along with any of his friends we can talk to."

"I like it," Drake agreed.

"What about Tressa? Do you think she'll go for it?" I hesitated near the passenger door.

"She'll probably go for anything we choose." Josh shrugged.

"You make an excellent point, young man." Kathleen halted on her way toward her car, hands on her hips. "Tressa wants to fit in and belong so much right now, that it could get her into some serious trouble. The woman who took Tressa home is her foster mom and she has three other kids at her place right now. It's not easy for a single lady to keep up with all of that. As an interpreter, I try to remove myself from the socialization, but don't think for a second, I won't call you all out on your behavior. We may be new here, but I have worked too hard to get her to where she is now. I won't have you three unraveling all those years and work. Understood?"

We all gave her a sheepish nod.

"Good." Kathleen's flats slapped the asphalt across the parking lot.

The boys parted ways.

Grandpa helped me open my door. He hooked a thumb toward Drake and Josh, "Those two seem nice. They sure do fight like siblings though."

"They're not related. Not even close."

Grandpa whistled most of the way home. I caught him looking at me every so often, snickering.

"Is it because I got into trouble?"

"Nope, it's because you finally threw the book at someone."

I giggled.

❖❖❖

The laptop on the kitchen counter was chiming when we walked through the door. I hurried over to it and answered, my backpack thumped the floor.

Mom and Dad's faces appeared.

"What took you so long? We've tried three times, I was about to call on the phone." Mom's brow furrowed. Dad teased her about the worry lines turning into wrinkles.

"Might as well get it over with." Grandpa strode into the kitchen and washed his hands. He pulled out a skillet, upending leftovers into it.

"Grandpa brought me home from school tonight." How long could I skirt the subject?

"This late?" Dad echoed Mom's concern. "There's nothing school related on my calendar."

"It was parent-teacher conferences, and . . ." Here it comes. "Grandpa also talked to the principal because I have in-school suspension for two days."

"What?"

I grimaced, the unison exclamation amplified through the speakers.

"I forgot that my yarn pouch had a book in it when I threw the yarn at two of my group mates to keep them from fighting. Thankfully, it was my bamboo circular knitting needles and they were tucked into the yarn ball."

"And that makes throwing things okay?" The screen froze a little, but it didn't hide Mom's red face.

"No, Ma'am."

It unfroze. "No yarn crafts for a week," Dad added.

"But…" I protested.

"Two weeks." He challenged. I kept my mouth shut.

"Be happy," Mom was on a roll. "That we're allowing you to keep your pleasure reading time."

Two weeks without knitting or crocheting. I'm gonna die.

"We actually called to say we're gone for another two weeks or more. Grandpa will have to enforce the yarn restriction." Dad cleared his throat. "Our time in Australia is up, but my hotshot crew is headed for California."

"Dispatch is sending me since I'm already out of the office." Mom wrote something down. My guess, her supply list for when they landed.

Dad's attention turned away at a knock on their hotel door. Mom left.

"Honey," she called, "The taxi's here."

"Love you. We'll call when we land stateside." The screen went black.

"Two whole weeks without yarn?" Grandpa set a steaming plate of food in front of me and held up a fork. "It's going to kill you."

I pushed food around my plate. "Tell me about it."

Chapter 8

Monica and I walked into the library. My first day back in the halls after surviving ISS purgatory.

Monica chided, "You're an old soul in a young person's body."

"No, I'm not. That's the weirdest thing I've ever heard." We put our backpacks in a corner of Mrs. Phelp's office.

"How many teens do you know agonize over not being able to crochet as punishment?" Monica rested her hands on her hips. She wore long black pants and a neon pink shirt with a Manga character on it. We moved to the checkout area of the desk.

"Lots did if there was a yarn shortage during the war." I started gathering books from the returns box underneath the counter.

Monica narrowed her eyes at me, "Which war?"

"World War II." Books landed with a thump on the counter. I sat in the tall stool to scan them back in.

"You referencing an older time period proves my point." The smirk on her face spoke victory.

I put my head on the counter and slapped it twice with my hand. "I'm not going to make it two weeks, it hasn't even been one yet."

"Die quietly, Amie. There are students trying to study." Mrs. Phelps said it in her sing-song way as she walked by pushing a cart of reference books for a class coming in soon.

I giggled.

"Much better, dear." She stopped in front of me on the other side of the counter. "Don't flatten anymore boys with books and you won't have to worry about it. I missed you."

She manipulated the cart with the squeaky wheel away from the desk. Mrs. Phelps reminded me of a cross between Morticia Addams, Mary Poppins, and Miss Frizzle. She was quite thin with straight, jet black hair. She even walked like Morticia Addams. Mrs. Phelps loved getting students to explore new and wacky things, like the time she caught a bunch of toads at a lake just to show us the variety of animal life there. No worries, she caught and released them with permission of the Department of Wildlife. Mrs. Phelps somehow came up with something unexpected.

"Face it, Amie. You're addicted to yarn." Monica patted my shoulder.

"No." I emphasized, "Yarn's addicted to me."

Monica snorted, "My mom has a Cricut, we should put the saying on a shirt."

"But what color would we get it in?" I tapped my chin.

"How about dark brown to match your eyes?" Pierce leaned on the counter. The swelling in his cheek had gone down, but faint green and brown markings tinged his face.

"Nah," I frowned. "What do you want?"

"My mom said I should be nice since we all could use more friends."

"Did she tell you this before our ISS or after?" My sarcasm dripped off every word. Monica came to my side.

Pierce shrugged, "I was only teasing before. Friends do that all the time. Catch ya later."

"That didn't sound like he's teasing," I muttered when he was out of hearing range. The scanner beeped every time I slid a barcode under the red laser. "Has he always been this weird?"

"No," Monica sighed. "He went to live with his mom last year. This is the most I've seen him, including being in school."

"Did you see his face?"

"What about it?" Monica started placing the books in order on the cart.

"His cheek was swollen before the ISS and today it has fading bruises on it."

"Oh, no. We should watch that. I'll talk to my dad when he gets back from his conference."

I opened a draft email and jotted down what we saw, the time, and location.

Chapter 9

ORCHARD MESA HIGH SCHOOL

"What, Mom? I'm about ready to walk into history class. Can't this wait until after school?" He answered his cell phone, someone jarring his elbow on their way by.

"Skunk, how dare you. You think school is more important than what I have for you to do? You know better." There was no reasoning with Mom when she got this way. "How's progress?"

She wanted an update? Now? Trained, by her, in counterintelligence and information gathering, she needed to go back to her manual. Granted his infiltration skills needed refining but, so far so good. "I'm working on it, but it's slow. Trust takes time, you taught me that."

"Don't get sassy with me." The line went dead. Another reminder of what he'd have to put up with when he got home.

He adjusted his backpack and walked into history class.

Chapter 10

Amie

MINING AND BOMBS. Tressa signed. Mrs. McCreedy let us have the last little bit of class to work on our projects. We all had some catching up to do. WHAT NEXT?

"I think we have to choose how we're going to present," Josh slowed down when he spoke so Kathleen could keep up with the conversation.

PAPER? I signed.

Tressa wrinkled her nose.

"No," Drake voiced.

"Performance?" Scanning the list of ideas, I looked around the group.

Drake rolled his eyes and Tressa said, MAYBE. Josh shrugged, but he grimaced.

"Documentary?"

Josh perked up, "Yes."

Drake frowned, "I'm not standing in front of a camera."

Tressa tilted her head to one side. Kathleen explained what it was. NO.

Drake thumbed through the packet. “All that’s left are the website and exhibit.”

“Let’s do website,” Josh beamed. Tressa and Kathleen started an animated conversation.

Drake frowned.

“It’s not fun being left out of a conversation, is it?” I raised my eyebrows, Drake focused on me.

“How are they even talking?” He watched the two.

“Ninety percent of what we say is body language. The deaf take it to a whole new level of artform and cool.” I smiled, but no one saw it.

Drake’s face went expressionless. Grandpa called it a poker face, but I’d never seen anyone use it outside of movies. I had no clue what he was thinking.

“Tressa doesn’t have internet at her house right now,” Kathleen explained.

“Everyone has internet,” Josh looked at Tressa weird.

“Not everyone, Josh.” Kathleen chided. “Her foster family is having trouble with the router or some wiring.”

Josh harrumphed and slouched in his seat. “So lame.”

SAME. Tressa signed.

“We have to do something everyone can join in on, unless you want to do it all, Josh.” I said throwing my hands up.

"Can't. I've got a project in science that's already doing that to me. I don't want another."

"D'you want to talk about it?" Tressa and I leaned forward.

Drake shook his head, "That's all girls ever want to do."

"No." Josh smiled at Drake, "I'll get over it, just not this minute."

"Okay, moving on… that leaves exhibit."

"Whatever." Josh punctuated it by checking the clock. "Class is almost over anyway."

"Mrs. McCreedy said we need to let her know next week about research assignments and who is doing what."

"We decided on uranium mining." Tressa gave Drake two thumbs up after Kathleen translated but he didn't look too sure about the gesture. "There's nothing more we need."

"What about the information available? Is there enough to research the topic?"

The bell rang.

"Have a good weekend everyone," Mrs. McCreedy stood at the door talking to the students filing out of class. Drake and Josh stood up and walked away. They were the same size and build. How come I never noticed this before?

"Guys," Neither turned around. "Hey."

I growled. Was this going to work?

Tressa motioned for my attention. MY NEW FAMILY GOING TO MINE TOMORROW.

WHERE? I put a pointer finger out and swished it right and left.

O-U-R-A-Y.

COOL. GOLD MINE THERE. I picked up my bag and followed her out the door.

Tressa pulled up beside me, MINE WE STUDY SAME.

MAYBE. All mines were tunnels in the ground, right? LEARN ALL YOU CAN. TELL ME MONDAY.

COOL. Tressa jumped up and down in the hall. Our exit was near. LATER.

SEE YOU LATER. I waved. Tressa pushed open the door and ran out to her mom's car.

"Having trouble with your group?" Pierce appeared out of nowhere. I jumped. "I could help you out."

"Thanks, but we'll figure something out." His hair was messier than usual. He patted it down a little, but it sprung back up. If he combed it, it may touch his shoulders.

"I'm doing mine on bomb manufacturing for the military, just in case you decide I can join your group."

"We aren't doing ours on bombs. Ours is on uranium."

"Bombs. Uranium. They go together. See ya." He left as fast as he came.

My stomach still felt off about the whole encounter when I walked into the house. Grandpa wasn't in the kitchen or the den. I followed the sound of his off-key singing to the garage. He was mounting a new spare tire on his truck. “Had to buy all new ones today. It’s a good thing Cecil had them in stock.”

“Wow. The flat was that bad?” I stopped beside him and watched him screw the spare in place.

“Found out the strangest thing about it.”

“What?”

The wrinkles in his face made his concern, look worse. “The flat was caused by someone slicing it with a knife.”

Chapter 11

"What?" I shrieked and gripped the side of the truck. The cold metal sent shivers up my spine. "At school, how is that possible?"

"I did make the rounds to all of your teachers and then to the principal to discuss your punishment." Grandpa dropped the tailgate so I could have a spot to sit. He sighed, "Someone had plenty of time."

"No one saw anything? I haven't heard a single thing on the gossip chain."

"Didn't know who to ask. But I did turn it in to the authorities. Now we wait and keep watch."

"That's it?" I searched his face, looking for a clue. Grandpa only stared out of the garage door. Did he really say that? Grandpa, the rescuer of lost teddy bears. The guy who knocked some man's front teeth out for trying to rob their mine. The same one the neighborhood tough guys steered clear of.

“Or,” the corner of Grandpa’s mouth hitched up. He picked up a bag from behind me and held it up. “We could install some high-tech gear and catch them the next time they try anything.”

“That’s more like it.” Grabbing the bag, I peered inside. A mishmash of electrical supplies collected at the bottom.

Grandpa bumped my arm, “Had you goin’ there for a minute, didn’t I.”

“You got me good.” I stirred the contents around. “Where’s the instructions?”

“Bah. Who needs instructions when you’ve got brains?” He popped open the first box and pulled out a long cable with a ball at the end. The cord snaked around his feet like spaghetti. “What’s this round thing?”

“The camera.” Grandpa cocked an eyebrow when I said it. “At least that’s what the picture shows.

"Kinda small to be takin’ video.” He gave it to me, removing a small black box that looked about the right size for storing the recordings. “Will this drive the car for me?

“No.”

“Good. I like telling my car what to do, not the other way around.” Grandpa scratched his head. He inspected the outside rear view mirror of the truck and ran his hand along the side. “This is going to be a fun adventure.”

Grandpa picked up a screwdriver off his small table, disconnected the side mirror and peered into the hole. “Everything’s supposed to go in there?”

I shrugged.

Grandpa reached into the bed of the truck. Plastic rustled and Grandpa removed zip ties from the store bag. He shook them at me, "I know what these do."

❖❖❖

Two hours later, I called Josh. He came over and I left Grandpa and Josh to their own devices.

Finding crumbs in the cookie jar, I set ingredients out to make more. Soon a batch of sugar cookies rested in the fridge to be baked later and I turned my attention to the chocolate chip batter. While Grandma lived, we learned how to substitute sugars in them. Sometimes I still did that.

The sweet gooey aroma of butter, sugar, and chocolate hung in the air. Arranging cooled cookies on a plate, I slid our glass door open and went to the detached garage. Josh's feet stuck out from underneath the truck. "That should do it, Grandpa."

The rest of Josh's body appeared, and he pulled himself up. He dusted the back of his pants off and smiled at the plate in my hand.

"You brought out cookies. Bless you." Grandpa kissed my forehead before taking some.

Josh reached over and grabbed a couple. "You can bake?" He grimaced. "I mean, um, good job not burning them."

"Thanks for doing this, Josh." Grandpa reached out and shook his hand. Red creeped up Josh's neck. He ignored me, mouth full of cookie and walked down the driveway. Josh rubbed the back of his neck, stopping at the front of the house to retrieve his bike.

Grandpa chuckled, "Amie, go pull him out of the hole he dug for himself." He absconded with the rest of the cookies and headed toward the house.

I jogged up. Words buzzed in my head. I scratched my hand, half wishing the rest of the group joined in, thankful they didn't. Not for this part anyway. "Hey, Josh."

He spewed the water he'd been drinking onto the concrete, "Yeah?"

"Thanks for the almost complement."

"Anytime." We stood there in awkward silence.

"Did you need something else?" Josh quipped, while he snapped the helmet strap and pulled his mountain bike upright.

"Don't tell anyone what you did to Grandpa's truck, okay? Thanks for coming."

"Sure. No problem." He slid on a pair of clear safety glasses and switched on the bicycle's front and rear lights. He glided the bike down the driveway. He rode up and over the boulder sized rock at the property line. "See ya, Monday."

Back inside, Grandpa enjoyed a cup of coffee with his cookie. I hooked the video receiver to an old computer monitor. The camera we installed in the truck recorded only when motion set it off. If anyone wanted to go after the truck again, we'd be ready for them. All video saved to an external drive. I rested my chin in my hand, waiting for the program to load.

Why go after a truck tire? Do truck tires translate to people being next? Did the video at the school have blind spots in it? Anyone paying attention had to observe something. It left several students off the list of suspects. None in detention had time or motive. Did they? Angry kids? Crazed adult?

The program finished loading and I opened it.

A video already?

It played. A shadow flitted across the screen.

The hairs on my arms stood up. My chest heaved, even as I sat.

A pink nose appeared on the monitor. I gasped. The neighbor's black cat inspected the lens.

I deleted it. Sighing.

Now to figure out why the tire got slashed in the first place.

Chapter 12

Dust particles danced when Grandpa opened the attic curtain.

"Why are we up here, Grandpa?" I fingered the lace on one of Grandma's unfinished doilies. My chest tightened. Oh, how I wished I'd asked her to teach me how to crochet lace before she died.

"You said you're researching uranium mining. You'll be able to look at some of it from up here." Grandpa rummaged through a stack of papers. Frowning, he shook his head and moved on to another box.

"But that stuff is out in the rafters of the garage." I toed the Christmas boxes.

"The work-related gear, yes. The paperwork however… Ah." He groaned as he lifted a large metal box, with a biohazard sign on the side, and set it on top of the ancient side table. Dust billowed out from its own nuclear fallout.

Grandpa flipped the latches and popped the lid. I craned my neck to see. A green ledger with red embossed lettering on the cover came out first. I pulled out a rusty, but locked, security box inside a plastic bag and set it aside.

A picture rested on the next layer of yellowing paperwork. A much younger version of Grandpa, in a hard hat with a dirt-smeared face, was flanked on both sides by two men. The black man on the left had a carefree smile that made his whole face beam. He made me want to get to know him. A scar parted his left eyebrow. The wiry European man with a hooked nose and beady eyes stood on Grandpa's right. He sneered. I cringed. This stranger oozed trouble.

"Who are these guys?" I held the picture up for Grandpa to see.

"Oh my," He set down the official embossed paper in his hand and took the picture, "It's been a long time since I've seen this."

He stilled. Grandpa's eyes misted and I placed my hand on his arm. He kissed the side of my forehead and left the attic.

What just happened? I wanted to follow him and ask a million questions, but I guess they could wait. Grandpa seemed to react that way a lot nowadays, needing moments by himself.

Turning back to the boxes, I found permits, certificates, and a bill of sale for a uranium mine. Dad said Grandpa and his partners had to sell to the bigger companies, but it didn't make any sense. Grandpa always supported small business owners. Why'd he sell out?

"The AEC," Grandpa's baritone voice right behind me made me jump. I imagined my head touching the bottom of the wooden beam on the roof. Okay. It didn't. But I sent dust bunnies scurrying around. Grandpa's deep laugh made his eyes dance. With my hand on my stomach, I willed the butterflies to calm down.

"The what?" I gulped.

"The Atomic Energy Commission made some decisions that put the bigger companies at an advantage to produce and mine uranium and turn a better profit than us little guys could. Made us small mining owners feel like we'd been jilted at the altar. We couldn't compete, so we sold out." He sniffled and cleared his throat. "It ended up being a providential time to get out too."

"Why?"

"The two guys in the photo mined that deadly yellow rock far longer than I did and paid the price for it. Both of 'em died from cancer. I keep waiting for my turn."

Grandpa could die? I know uranium is dangerous stuff to handle, but. . . Would that mean Mom and Dad would take me with them, or would we move somewhere else again? What about school? Who'd hang out with Tressa or talk books with Monica? And Grandpa. Who'd be there to tease me about eating cookie dough?

“Don’t worry,” Grandpa pulled me into a hug. He seemed to be really good at reading my thoughts. “I keep a yearly check with my doctor on the books.”

I grimaced the world’s worst grin.

“Amie, I’m fine. I’m not planning on going anywhere anytime soon. Come on,” he released me and nudged my arm. “Your parents should be in California now. Let’s see if they’re on. It’ll be easier to keep track of the time zone.”

I paused before descending the attic ladder. We made a mess of dust and paperwork. A few sheets cascaded off of the side table and onto the floor. I’d be back for it later.

Chapter 13

TEMPERATURE STAYS AROUND 50 DEGREES, Tressa signed while Kathleen voiced. VERY COOL. I WANT GO AGAIN.

Josh grinned. Drake's poker face seemed to solidify his expression into a bored statue every time we started a conversation. What was up with him?

BOTH MINES SAME? Tressa shrugged, glancing around the table to see if we knew the answer.

DON'T KNOW. I opened my history notebook and added the question to the now growing list of important things to find. My hand cramped up, I shook it, looking to Kathleen for help.

She motioned for me to continue.

"We need to break up the tasks since we only have a few months and not much time to work on this in class." No one seemed to object or say anything at all. I plunged on with, "Tressa, you should answer the questions about how mines worked since you visited one."

She sat taller in her chair.

"Josh, what about finding out the technologies they used in the mines?"

Josh cleared his throat, "I read up on the specifications for the exhibit also. We can get creative with it. I thought of maybe using a dump truck or conveyor belt that can move with all of the information on it."

"I like it." I beamed and checked on Drake, the oh-so-moody one next to me. He acknowledged it with a bend of his neck.

"We still need a general history of the uranium boom," I sighed, massaging at the knot in my hand.

"And a personal touch," Drake reminded us.

"Maybe Grandpa will let us use some of his stuff. Like the hard hat," Josh rubbed his hands together and Tressa nodded, excitement brightening her face. "Does he have more cool gear?"

"Grandpa showed me some paperwork from his mining days, and he promised later to pull out some of his old equipment. He showed me an old picture of him and his partners. He's secretive about it though. Some memories seem difficult for him to chat about. The other two are both dead now."

SPIES? J-A-M-E-S B-O-N-D? Tressa leaned in.

Drake flinched. "If you can get me their names, I'll look them up. I've done some genealogy research and it's pretty easy to find people.

"Wow. Um. Okay." I paused. "I'm not sure how soon I'll be able to drag that information out of him."

Josh sniggered.

"What," Drake narrowed his gaze at Josh. "You don't think I know how to run a computer or open a book?"

"Nope. I thought you were a vicious, knuckle dragger."

Tressa put her arms down at her sides and hunched her back, her lower jaw jutted out. Josh doubled over laughing.

The bell rang. The air crackled around Drake. His eyes spit sparks and his face tinged red.

"Dumb girl," he mouthed and rocketed out of the classroom. Tressa paled.

My heart thundered in my chest, "Drake." Shoving books and notebooks into my bag, I hurried after him.

I pushed into the congested hall, trying to skirt around people to catch up to him. Drake's long legs gave him an advantage. Bouncing between high schoolers, I ricocheted off a linebacker and almost tripped over my own feet on the outside stairs. Drake stalked over to the bicycle rack.

"Hey," I shouted. "What's up with you?" Stomping to the other side of his bike, I faced him with the rack between us. Other students gave us side glances while getting their own locks open.

"She started it," Drake fumbled with his U-lock, not quite getting the key in.

"Josh did. Tressa only added to the visual. American Sign Language is all visual and comes out brash and blunt."

Little dots danced behind my eyes, matching the rhythm of my heart. My blood pressure must be reaching terminal velocity. Part of me wanted to take Drake's head off.

He gripped the top of the bike rack and leaned over so close our noses almost touched. "A joke at my expense," he growled.

"She's only trying to fit in. It's not easy to do when no one understands what you're saying."

"And you're defending her," his voiced cracked at the end and something shifted in his expression. It reminded me of a Japanese porcelain doll I saw in a museum with Grandma once. The face had shattered at some point and they melded all the cracks together with gold. They highlighted the beauty of imperfections. Drake's face hadn't been put back together yet.

All the air went out of my lungs, and my heart slowed. The key went into the lock, but Drake's shoulders sagged. He stood there frozen.

What's going on with him? He's been here long enough for the new kid syndrome to be out of his system. Right?

"Someone has to, because not many people will." Couldn't we just research, without all the fighting?

"I'll take Drake's spot in the group," Pierce sauntered up, scratching his shoulder.

"No," we both said together. Drake gave me a shocked look. We hadn't agreed on much, but this, it seemed we did.

"Mrs. McCreedy said the groups are now etched in stone. There's no changing." I hoped Pierce would go away.

"It was worth a try," Pierce turned and headed up the sidewalk. Why the rush to join us all the time?

"Great," Drake watched him go. "I'm stuck in it for the duration."

"Friends stick up for each other, they tease each other, and apologize when things go wrong." What could I add?

"I will, when she will."

Chapter 14

ORCHARD MESA HIGH SCHOOL SIDEWALK

Why wouldn't anyone stick up for him? What did that feel like? Doomed to always be the outcast? No one knew the skills he had.

He rubbed a hand on his chest. The lonely ache returned, like someone took a chunk out of his chest and nothing around could fill the hole.

No one wanted him. They also wouldn't see him cry or mope. He'd make it with or without them. Tough to the end.

His jaw still hurt, a normal pain. Life turned out to be messier than he ever thought. Infiltrating this group proved harder than his mom claimed it'd be. He needed the information back before they figured out what they possessed. Their research project, perfect. It made his job finding it simple.

Would Amie ever count him as a friend too? Did he deserve it?

Chapter 15

Amie

The drama was going to kill me. My shoes slapped the floor more than usual. I entered the classroom once more to find the rest of my group where I left them.

Tressa gestured her frustration. Flopping down into my seat with my back to the door, Tressa motioned through several expletives. “You don’t have to voice those ones, Kathleen.”

Tears dribbled down Tressa’s chin and she buried her face into her hands.

“So I’m learning all of the cuss words first?” Josh’s gaze bounced around, not sure who to settle on.

“Pretty much.” Weight pressed down on my shoulders.

Mrs. McCreedy glided over to us. “What happened?”

“Some teasing got out of control,” I sighed. The burden digging itself in to stay.

"That's usually what teasing leads to." Mrs. McCreedy dropped into Drake's vacant seat and knocked gently on the desks.

Tressa sniffled and looked up. Her face turned pink when she saw our teacher.

TELL ME, Mrs. McCreedy pointed to herself. She'd sign a couple of things to Tressa every day.

Kathleen helped voice, "We were making jokes and Josh called Drake a jock. Lots of fun. I acted it out. Drake called me dumb and left. I'm not dumb, I can speak. I choose not too. Signing's easier."

"How did that make you feel?" Mrs. McCreedy never looked at Kathleen, only Tressa.

Tears rolled down Tressa's face. I left and brought the tissue box back. BAD, she signed.

"What Drake did wasn't kind. He also plays a sport that isn't as popular as football. Drake doesn't really like football. If he had his choice, he'd rather watch soccer. How do you think he felt when you teased him?"

Tressa looked down at the desk and shrugged after Kathleen finished signing.

I didn't know Drake preferred soccer over football.

How did she find that out? No wonder he felt stuck.

"Did Drake laugh *with* you and Josh?" Mrs. McCreedy pointed to Josh who winced.

Tressa frowned in concentration. She looked up at the ceiling a minute, then back at Mrs. McCreedy. NO. She made the same face Drake did before he left. FACE PINK.

"Both of you were hurt, right?" Mrs. McCreedy waited.

Tressa nodded.

"How are we going to fix that hurt?"

Tressa thought a minute and looked at Josh and I for the answer. Neither of us said anything. Josh rubbed a hand across his chest.

TELL SORRY, Tress suggested.

Mrs. McCreedy nodded, "Drake, I'd like to see you at my desk. We need to talk."

Swiveling in my chair, I found Drake standing at the threshold of the door. His wary stride took him to Mrs. McCreedy's desk, where she met him. Their backs to us.

Tressa bumped my elbow, WHAT SAY?

CAN'T HEAR, I answered.

Drake's hands were stuffed in his pant pockets. His shoulders slumped, he rocked back and forth on his feet. Mrs. McCreedy leaned over her desk and I saw the flash of a sticky note. She handed it to Drake and patted his shoulder. He leaned over the desk and wrote something, then walked over to us, the cheerful yellow note stuck to his left index finger. Drake attached it to the desk in front of Tressa.

I'm sorry.

Tressa studied Drake's face. The anger vanished, but he also didn't meet her gaze. Tressa cleared her throat and Drake looked at her. I SORRY, Tressa signed, and Kathleen voiced it.

Drake let out a sigh and held out his hand.

The weight I carried lifted.

Tressa moved closer and pumped his hand. He bobbed his head once and exited the room.

Chapter 16

"Well," Grandpa paused, his arm draped along the back of the front porch swing we rocked in. It creaked before swinging the other direction. Dry leaves knocked against tree limbs and skittered across the street. "It sounds like you had a long day."

I exhaled a slow breath, "Keeping a group together isn't easy."

"Is it meant to be easy?"

"Huh. You have a way of putting things into perspective." I leaned my head on his shoulder.

"That's my job." He hesitated and pulled the picture from the attic out of his shirt pocket. We both stared at it. He pointed to the African American on the left.

"Joe Billings was a great guy." Grandpa's voice came out thick, his eyes glistened with unshed tears. "He pulled me out of scrapes, and I helped him out of a few. It tore him up the most when we had to sell the claim. If it wasn't for him, I'd never have met your grandma."

"How'd you meet?"

He cleared his throat and contemplated the ceiling, not really looking at the awning. Grandpa still found it hard to share stories about Grandma. I waited for him to get the story out. "Joe and I were ice fishin' on the Mesa. We were packing it in for the day when I slipped and landed on the open tackle box. Hooks, tackle line, bait covered my thigh and bit into my flesh." Grandpa scratched his head. "And a few found my hind end."

I snickered, trying to swallow my smile. He gave me a playful shove.

"How did that help you meet Grandma? She wasn't a nurse." Curling my feet up under me, Grandpa moved his arm, rotated it and flexed his fingers. He played with the wedding band he still wore.

"No, she worked as a receptionist at a factory."

"Then how'd Joe help you meet?" I put my nose near Grandpa's shoulder.

"Slow down. One thing at a time." Did his face tinge pink? He stared into my eyes.

"You have to finish the story now."

"Limping out of the emergency room, I saw her. She was beautiful." The corner of Grandpa's mouth hitched up. "Grandma had come up to see how a worker fared after getting his hand caught in a machine. Joe could tell I was smitten, but he also knew I was embarrassed about getting caught in the tackle. Good thing for me, Joe didn't have a shy bone in his body. He walked up to her and said, 'Ma'am, my buddy Ed wants to say hi, but he isn't thinking to swift right now. Whatever they used to numb his leg slowed his brain down.' The rest is history."

I roared. My stomach hurt from laughing so much. Grandpa chuckled too.

Inhaling, I pointed to the more sinister one on the right, "What about the other guy?"

"That's Pags. He broke his nose in a bar fight. Didn't help his looks any. Always a shadowy one. Neither of us felt he was completely trustworthy, but he helped start the claim, so what could we say?"

"Pags?"

"Yeah. Never could say his whole last name very well when we needed his attention quick. An odd duck, that one." Grandpa tilted his head to the side.

"How?" I inched forward. I enjoyed every minute of this.

"The guy acted pretty secretive. Always in trouble with a fight or another miner. Preferred to be in people's business but somehow made it look as if he avoided it. Every once in a while, he'd sneak off and poke around other people's claims."

My inner radar perked up. This might be the lead we need for our research. "What was his whole name? Drake is an expert name finder."

“Pags died, Amie. He’s buried in the cemetery down the road.” Grandpa squinted at me.

“Maybe we can leave flowers at his grave.” I needed a more convincing line than that.

“Amie,” He used his you’re-going-to-be-in-trouble growl. “Spill the beans.”

“I need a human face on our research. Weaving in the personal story will get people more engaged than just researching mining. Not random facts they have to string together. Please.” Clasping my hands under my chin, I begged.

“Not if you beg,” Grandma clenched his jaw. I tromped over sensitive territory. And Grandpa never liked admitting I had him wrapped around my pinky. I sat straight up and watched him turn the picture around in his hand. Would he let me wade into the hurting places of his heart?

He stared at the picture of the three of them for a long time. The stress of the day seeped out of my bones with each sway of the swing. I blinked, each time my eyes stayed closed a little longer.

Grandpa nudged me, a smirk plastered across his face. “You fell asleep and you snore.”

“I do not.” How could he say that about me?

“Sleep or snore?” He beamed, his wrinkles scrunching his blue eyes.

“You know what I mean.”

“I dunno, my brain ain’t what it used to be.”

"Snore. I don't snore."

"How would you know?" The swing shifted when he stood. "Do you stay awake to find out?"

Grandpa handed me the photo and went inside. The screen door banged.

I flipped the picture over and found their names printed on the back. The one I needed scrawled across the bottom.

Leon Paglione.

Chapter 17

“Drake, Drake, Drake,” I waved him over to the library door since I needed to get on the desk. With lunch finished, students milled around on their way to the next class. Drake angled away from me, but I didn’t give him a chance. Grabbing his wrist, I yanked him through the doors. “I have a name.”

“Congratulations?” His abrupt halt disconnected us. He squinted at me. “Did you forget it over the weekend?”

“No. My grandpa gave me a picture of him and his two friends and their names are on the back. You did say you’d look up names, right?”

A lightbulb of understanding registered on Drake’s face. “Great.” It came out flat. He stuffed his hands deep in the pockets of his jeans.

Not to be deterred, I looped my hand through his elbow and dragged him the remainder of the way to the checkout counter. Only student workers were allowed behind the desk, I heard a sigh come from him when I left him standing in front of the divider. Ducking into Mrs. Phelps' office, I deposited my bag and found the CD case with the picture tucked in between a couple of books. Keeping it safe, my top priority.

Drake tugged at his shirt collar. He rubbed the back of his neck, looking uncertain when I came back out of the office.

"You okay?" I slid the jewel case toward him.

"Fine," he half snarled.

He didn't sound fine to me, but I let it slide. "I can't let you take the photo with you, but you could take a photo of a photo." I smiled.

"Good idea." Drake popped open the CD case and gently rotated the picture on both sides when he took the photos. With the same care, he closed the jewel case and handed it back.

"How fast do you think you can find anything?" I prodded.

Drake shrugged, "It depends on what we're looking for and if anything is on the searches I use."

"How about headstones, birth and death dates?"

He raised his shoulders again.

"What's up with you today? I know you aren't the world's greatest conversationalist, but something's wrong. Start talking."

"I have a lot on my mind. There's a big qualifying race coming up for a state spot." He refused to meet my eyes.

"BMX, right?"

"Yeah."

"Drake, what else is it? A big race is like a big test. While it makes you nervous, it isn't anything to shut down over. This is… I dunno… different." He avoided my gaze. "Come on. I don't normally bite."

"But you do throw books." He gave me a half smile and shifted his weight. He opened his mouth to say something, then snapped it closed. Sighing, "Lot of pressure at home."

"The library is a great place to escape."

Surprise mingled with apprehension, but Drake followed me to a study area. On the way there, I detoured and grabbed one of the bicycle books off the shelf. I put it on the table and Drake lowered himself into the chair. He thumbed through it and set it back down.

He glared at me. I moved to the side, but Drake's eyes didn't follow me.

No. Not at me. Around me.

Pierce stood at the checkout counter.

I pasted on a smile, "What can I help you with Pierce?"

"Monica said something about easy Shakespeare." He didn't want to be here either.

"I know exactly where that it is. Mrs. Phelps has a whole section of Shakespeare's plays in graphic novel format." Yanking on Pierce's arm, I dragged him to Drake's table. A quick trip to the class literature section and I had the book sitting in front of Pierce in no time.

Pierce jumped away from it.

“It’s not a spider, Pierce. You don’t have to be afraid of it.” This kid needs professional help.

“Who told you I’m afraid of spiders?” Pierce demanded.

“No one. It was only an example. You’re jumpy.”

“What’s it to you?” Pierce crossed his arms over his chest.

“Who cares what you’re afraid of?” Walking toward the desk I called over my shoulder, “Books can sometimes help with that too.”

Chapter 18

ORCHARD MESA HIGH SCHOOL LIBRARY

He and the other kid had a glaring contest. Not Amie's smartest idea, seating them at the same table, but she didn't understand the rivalry.

He sighed and picked up the book. Amie's kindness meant a lot.

How much more could he take from his mom? His job was simple. Infiltrate the group, find the information, and leave. What about the weird feelings that came with it? While he didn't belong anywhere and no one wanted him as a friend, he no longer desired to hurt the others and vanish. He'd done this at so many schools already. He had the perfect cover for getting at personal information.

Who would ever suspect a kid?

Even if he faced rejection, he'd never been this close to someone caring.

Fingering the pages, he let his gaze wander to the other side of the table. The other kid frowned and moved his mouth while reading. As a possible threat, he'd keep an eye on him. This one had potential to ruin everything.

Get the information, get out, move on. Don't get beaten to death. Right.

His ribcage twinged in pain, sore from last night's thrashing. Why did it always have to be his side?

He could do this.

He opened the book, page 1.

Chapter 19

Amie

Tressa and I stood at the pick-up curb near the parking lot of Orchard Mesa High School. We both leaned on her foster mom's car. The dark patches under her light brown eyes had gone and her dishwater blond hair curled out of a ponytail. Her eyes crinkled at the edges when she smiled. Tressa stared at me, I listened to the cell phone at my ear continue to ring.

"You get detention again, Scamp?" Grandpa's laugh carried through the phone.

"Thanks for your vote of confidence." Shaking my head, I waited for him to stop chortling. "Can Tressa spend the night on Friday?"

HE ASK IF WE IN TROUBLE AGAIN. I signed. Tressa smirked.

"I don't see why not." In my mind I saw him scratching his head like he always did when thinking. "What's Tressa's parents say?"

"You can talk with Tressa's mom and leave me out of the middle." I handed the phone over.

Cars zoomed out of the parking lot. A few honked at us for inconveniencing them. Trucks sent out throaty growls. Students fled the confines of the school and three big yellow busses pulled away from the curb.

Drake and Josh exited the building to collect their bikes and set to unhooking their high valued property. Josh's mountain bike stood taller with tires meant to grip the soft dirt. Drake's sat lower, and built for speed. Both had brand stickers pasted on them.

Tressa moved to my side and we both watched them chat.

CAN YOU SEE WHAT THEY SAY? I nudged her.

NO, TOO FAR. NEED…she made two circles with her hands and put them up to her face. I made binoculars with my own hands and stared into her eyes too. We giggled.

Josh's head tilted back and his stomach moved in a laugh. At least they are on speaking terms for now. They low fived each other and bumped knuckles. Friends? They rode off in opposite directions.

Football players jogged out to the field for practice. There's a big game this weekend. It's homecoming, but I don't care. Not that anyone would ask me. Too gawky. No dancing skills. The marching band warmed up near the school. They have a competition coming soon, I think. Other students walked off campus, headed in all sorts of directions. Grandpa likes me to walk as long as the weather is nice. He says the fresh air clears my brain. It does.

Tressa bumped my elbow. I returned my focus on her. She wiggled her eyebrows and her grin curled in a way that spelled out trouble. WHICH BOY YOU LIKE? D-R-A-K-E? J-O-S-H?

NONE, I answered. YOU LIKE J-O-S-H.

Tressa sighed and placed her hands over her heart. YEAH.

"That sounds good to me too," Tressa's foster mom handed me back my phone.

"Thanks," I put the phone to my ear. "You still there, Grandpa?"

"Yep. Tressa's family will be gone this weekend, anyway. She's able to come over if I understood it right."

"What's not to get?" Tressa and her mom went into deep conversation.

"Something about respite care. She's going to talk with Tressa's case worker." Grandpa paused, "If it does work out, Tressa's overnight bag will be at home by the time you get out of school and both you girls can walk home together."

"Totes!" Tressa turned to watch my minor happy dance.

"What?" The confusion in Grandpa's voice is evident.

"Uh." I ducked my head a little, "That's great, Grandpa. See you in a little bit." I ended the call.

MAYBE. Tressa signed.

HOPE, I replied.

Chapter 20

School today ended up as one of those topsy-turvy sort of schedules because of an assembly for homecoming. Tressa and I would be eating Greek food. Way more fun than a dance, any day, according to Tressa. I agreed.

My time in the library landed in the morning instead of the afternoon. Not that I minded, library time any part of the day was fine with me. I pulled the book return box on wheels out from its hiding spot under the book drop. The books Drake and Pierce looked through yesterday mixed in somewhere. Stacking them next to the computer, Monica started to check them in. Neither of us talked much. Sleep still held us in its clutches, even if we had to be awake.

About the time I had halfway finished pushing the unwieldy book catch back into its proper place, a student walked by on the way out of the library and dropped a book down the return slot.

Thump.

"Thanks a lot," I mumbled.

Monica snickered.

"It'd be less funny if you were the one spelunking for books," I huffed

"But I'm not, so it's hilarious," She made no effort to hide her toothy grin.

Disappearing under the counter, I attempted to crawl around without moving anything. The corner of the recycle and paper container jabbed me in the ribs. "Ouch."

"I think the recycle bin goes by the door," Monica's voice was muffled.

"Why?" My head bumped against the front wall of the checkout station.

"It's always there when we come in the library." She sounded closer. Did she lean over?

"Is there a morning checklist? Is it different from our after lunch one?" Pushing the recycle box out, I nailed my elbow on the edge of the book return cart. My complaint went unheard. I knew I should've moved it out further before getting down.

"Found it. One of the morning crew left a sticky note. We need to move them."

"Now she tells me." I shook off what I hoped wouldn't turn into a bruise and pressed on. No turning back now, no matter what monsters lurked under there.

"What'd you say?" The little light I had disappeared.

"Can you move the book return?"

"Not unless you want it to go four-wheeling over your leg." The oversized box moved and bumped my leg.

"Thanks anyway."

The light returned and glinted off a shiny piece of metal. I twisted and found a delicate necklace caught on the lower corner of the return slot. The fragile chain snagged on a gap where the corners joined. A gentle tug left it dangling from my fingers. "I found that girl's necklace."

"Yay," Monica declared, and the eruption of clacking computer keys made me smirk. That girl probably received a lost and found email.

I dragged myself and the necklace out after retrieving the book. Misjudging the distance, I whacked the back of my head on the underneath side of the counter. "Really? Ugh."

Feeling around for the counter, I grabbed it and pulled myself up only to come back down on one knee, an avalanche of books sliding into my face. In true ninja form, my arms flailed to catch tomes only to send them flying all over the area behind the desk.

Between fits of giggles, Monica managed to ask, "Are you okay?" Tears pooled at the corners of her eyes.

Mrs. Phelps appeared, "Amie?" She relaxed after she surveyed the disaster. "Try to survive the remainder of the day."

"Yes, ma'am." My shoulders slumped and I set off, still on my knees, to create order from my chaos. Drake and

Pierce's books launched the farthest. Both rested open against each other. I hope I didn't break a spine. A folded piece of paper sitting nearby could only be from one of their books. Any scrap of paper I found served as a bookmark. I'd return someone's homework in class today. Picking it up, I saw my name on it. I gasped at the note inside.

"Monica," I rasped out. She read from behind me.

Dear Amie,

Thanks for the book.

You should stay away from Drake, I wouldn't trust him. He's shady.

His mom is mean, his dad is distant, and he's caught in the middle of something that won't end well. It's safer to give him a cold shoulder and kick him out of the group before everyone gets hurt. Especially your grandpa. Things are already heavy handed at home and it would be bad for everyone else to feel that level of wrath from my mom.

Get out while you still can.

Skunk

"Whoa," Monica breathed out. "Pierce's mom beats him? I need to tell Dad and Mom. I know he's a jerk, but maybe he's trying to compensate for all of the junk going on in his life."

"What about Drake?" I asked.

"Having weird parents isn't a crime. We'd all be in trouble. But Pierce." His name died on Monica's tongue. Her eyes watered.

I hugged her, "That's scary. We've got to tell someone."

Chapter 21

Finally, Friday. My shoes slapped the concrete on the walk home. I exhaled. I hadn't gotten Pierce off of my mind the rest of the week. Monica talked with her parents about it and they decided to contact child protective services. A tricky situation for sure. People may end up thinking Monica's family created a power play to ruin his mom's life. That's how she would see it. Did Pierce hate Drake that much? Why was Pierce pushing so hard to be in the group? Jealousy? Would he get help in time?

A hand yanked my arm. Straightening my gaze, a tree flashed into my view, inches from my face.

Tressa frowned and shook her head at me. NOT LISTENING. YOU.

SORRY.

She lifted her hands and let them drop.

THINKING ABOUT PIERCE. I needed to refocus.

SKUNK FACE? Starting at her forehead, Tressa pulled the letter K along the top of her scalp and then used her pointer finger and circled her face.

I nodded and explained about the note, which weighed like lead in my backpack. Who do I give it to?

MAYBE SKUNK, P-I-E-R-C-E, NOT OK. BUT NO WISH THAT ON HIM. MAYBE HE FIND GOOD HOME. NOT MINE. BUT DIFFERENT.

Pierce had a long way to go before Tressa would allow herself to trust him. WE CAN HOPE.

We both turned up my driveway and went through the front door porch area. Tressa liked the swing. I slammed into her when she stopped abruptly through the door. She ignored me and smelled the air. Grandpa had found lamb. Tressa went into a happy dance. We dropped our school gear in a chair and she followed me to the kitchen. After washing our hands, she crowded into Grandpa's space in front of the stove. Pots and pans awaiting for the next step in the process.

GOOD JOB? BAD JOB? Grandpa signed worry creased his brow.

Tressa wrapped her arms around him.

Grandpa's face melted into a half smile and he patted her back. GOOD. WHAT NEXT?

Tressa inched him out of the way and began putting rice and meat into grape leaves with the flourish of a professional at work. She wrote instructions to start things, but now she turned into the champion of the kitchen. Rolled grape leaves went into a pot of boiling water with a plate and rock to weigh it down. We unearthed and cleaned a medium stone, an important ingredient, which added the flavor of tradition to the process.

The pile of grape leaves on a plate grew into a beautiful mound. Saliva filled my mouth.

We moved everything to the small kitchen table for four and sat down. Tressa interlaced her fingers on the table and looked at Grandpa. He'd bitten into one of the grape leaves. It was like a green spring roll from the Asian restaurants, but filled with different things. His eyes were closed and a slow, satisfied smile spread across his face. Opening his eyes, he stopped mid-chew when he saw us staring at him.

WHAT? Grandpa shrugged.

PRAY? Tressa asked and tilted her head to wait.

LONG TIME AGO. Grandpa motioned.

NO PROBLEM. GOOD TIME, START NOW.

Grandpa prayed? How long had it been? He'd never brought it up and we never go to church.

Tressa pointed to me.

I DON'T KNOW HOW. YOU?

I LEARN. Tressa responded. MOM TEACH ME WHEN I ASK. FEELS WEIRD, BUT GOOD.

OH I SEE. I wondered if my face looked like a prune with how confused I felt. Grandpa gave me a wink.

Auntie used to pray a lot. I snuck into her room all the time to watch her daily dance. She never acknowledged my presence. I always left before she finished. She signed to God like He was in the room. I never felt brave enough to ask if God ever talked back. Is that possible? Does God sign?

Grandpa stretched his spine straighter and looked at the ceiling. THANK YOU, LORD FOR TODAY. THANK YOU FOR T-R-E-S-S-A, A-M-I-E. FOR FRIENDS AND FOOD. AMEN.

Tressa held her hand flat, palm up and bounced a thumbs up sign into it.

I followed. AMEN.

Tressa nodded and took a couple of grape leaf rolls off the platter.

I did too. A taste of heaven in my mouth.

WHAT YOU TWO DO AFTER DINNER? Grandpa asked. The nice part about ASL, no one got in trouble for speaking with their mouth full.

MOVIE? Tressa's eye lit up and she pasted on a smile.

DON'T BEG. I warned.

Tressa frowned in an effort to not smile, but it only made her face take on a weird mix of excited and grumpy.

Grandpa chuckled. FINE.

I popped up and kissed his cheek. Tressa kissed the other one.

THANKS, GRANDPA. Tressa squeezed his neck.

After we ate, I collected the now empty dishes and took them to the sink to prepare them for the dishwasher. Reaching for the faucet handle, it surprised me when Grandpa's hand covered my own. "Go on, Scamp. It's a girl's night. Let me do this part."

"Thanks." Grandpa didn't give me any time to respond but bumped my hip with his own to nudge me out of the way.

We went into the den and opened the movie cupboard. Tressa combed through the movies, pulling out several to read the back covers. In the end, she picked a cartoon movie. I turned the volume off and the closed captions on. Tressa and I curled up on the couch under the blankets.

We were half-way through the movie when my cell phone sounded and Tressa's vibrated. Grandpa trudged by on his way up the stairs toward his room.

Unknown Number: Amie.

Me: Who's this?

Unknown: Drake.

Me: How'd U get my #?

Drake: Josh

Me: I'm busy.

Tressa pushed my shoulder and showed me her phone screen. Josh had texted her too.

Josh: Tressa, bring Amie and meet us at the cemetery.

US? I looked at Tressa and she shrugged.

My phone buzzed. Drake: Not too busy for this.

Me: Try me.
Drake: Leon Paglione has 2 graves.

Chapter 22

"I can't believe I'm doing this," I groaned as I slowed my mom's bike to a stop at the cross street to turn left on Unaweep Avenue. Riding double with Tressa sitting on the seat while I peddled standing up, proved challenging. Why mom chose a girl's bike with a basket on the front, I'll never know. She's more of the mountain biking type. I liked it, because I carried my library books in it.

Stars twinkled in the expanse above us. The lights flickered on the streetlamps every so often. Tressa squeezed my sides, pinching where her fingernails dug in. I rotated to check on her and the bike wobbled. Her face was etched with worry. I slowed down to check.

YOU SURE? WE CAN GO BACK RIGHT NOW.

Tressa shook her head. ADVENTURE.

We're going to die. I rode a bike in the dark with a friend who's deaf. The blind used their ears, the deaf used their eyes. Sticking Tressa in the dark technically meant I had now made her blind too. Sighing, I began to turn the bike back toward my house.

Tressa grabbed my arm. WE PROMISED.

YOU CAN'T SEE. At least we had a little light right now.

She gulped, YOU MY EYES.

NOT WORTH TROUBLE TO ONLY FIT IN. I WORRIED FOR YOU.

MOM SAY, HAVE FINISH PROMISE.

NO. NOT THIS. I put my hands on my head.

TEAM TOGETHER.

My shoulders slumped. FINE.

TRUST YOU WITH MY EYES.

We resettled and I switched on my front headlight. Tressa returned to digging her nails in my sides and I pushed off. We gained speed on the quiet street and I rolled into the bicycle lane. We passed houses with TVs on, the middle school, and the bowling alley with a car packed parking lot. It must be league night. My burning legs got a rest when we coasted down the hill to the stop light, the brakes protesting at us for riding double. We had to go back up the hill to get home.

NEED PUSH BUTTON. Tressa steadied the bike while I raced over to push the crosswalk button. A few drivers gave us strange looks when we rode across the four-lane highway. I puffed hard past the headstone engravers. The darkness engulfed us.

Death's whisper left an eerie stillness in the air. The bicycle tires crunched and cracked over the old asphalt, pine needles, and dried leaves. We passed under the iron banner of Calvary Cemetery and its stone pillared entryway. I slowed the bike to a crawl and we both got off. My sides were going numb where Tressa gripped me, and her breath was now hot on my neck. Bare branches knocked against each other.

A hand grabbed me, my shriek echoed a call to raise the dead. I balled my fist and lashed out. The bike clattered to the ground.

"Hey. Hey. It's me, Josh." He moved the light up toward his chin, laughing.

"That's not funny." I yelled in his face. Tressa wrapped her arms around my mid-section and I squeezed her arm.

Josh backed up. Another beam joined his, forcing me to shield my face. The second light redirected toward the concrete.

My heart refused to slow down.

"You okay?" Drake stopped several feet away, his face shrouded in shadow. He gave me a wary look.

"No," I gasped. "Tressa can't hear and now she's blinded by the lack of light too. Meeting in the cemetery after dark, worst idea ever. We can get in a lot of trouble, you know."

"Oh." Josh sobered up and moved toward Tressa. "Sorry, Amie."

"I'm fine," I retorted.

Josh signed, HORSE RIDE?

I saw Tressa's face turn red even in the dim light, but she glowed at the same time. He leaned down and she hopped on his back.

I leaned my bike against a tree. The chain had slipped off. Great. Now we get to walk home in the dark. Josh led us through the maze of headstones.

"We already found the first one," Drake skirted around a large headstone. His flashlight glinted off his polished dress shoes.

"Boring date at Homecoming?" Did he talk to other girls? Did I care?

"No. I needed a cover to get in and use a computer." Drake stated.

"They close that part of the school off for dances and other functions." I countered.

"Coach left his office unlocked with a little help today. It's not that far from the gym," he added.

Who was this guy?

We'd caught up to Josh, who stared at a headstone flush with the ground. The wrinkled coat of his tux straightened when Tressa slid off of his back and inspected the stone. Did the boys plan it together or was it a random meeting of the minds?

"This is Pags' official headstone," Drake explained.

Leon Paglione's headstone only had a death date. No clues to how he died. Grandpa said it best, no one loved him enough to know him. He pushed people away.

Like Drake.

My chest tightened. "Where's the other one?" My voice cracked.

Tressa looked at me. I pulled Drake's arm enough so she could see me in the light. His gaze guarded, Drake left the light where I directed.

OFFICIAL ONE.

"Pauper's Field," Josh added.

I pointed toward the way we rode in so Tressa would know what to expect next.

Drake killed the light. Tressa gasped. I started to protest when Drake's hand went over my mouth. The distinct sound of a shovel hitting a rock vibrated through the air.

Drake let go and gripped my arm. Josh and Tressa teamed up again and we all scurried over to the wooden picket fence separating the cemeteries.

We froze. The shush of dirt moving filled the stillness.

"Did you hear that?" A male voice whispered. How did they not see or hear us from earlier? I know I wasn't silent. Did they only just arrive?

A clang sounded, followed by the shuffling of feet over grass. They ran off.

We moved to where they dug moments before. Drake spread his hand over the light and pointed it at the ground so not as much would escape. A three-foot-long and two-foot deep hole in the ground, meant they didn't hear me or were very fast moles. Nothing to see besides footprints. They hadn't dug deep or wide enough to unearth a casket. What were they looking for?

Drake bent over and picked up the shovel. "This is my shovel," he whispered.

"How?" I squeaked.

"I don't know. Pierce trailed me part of the way home today, but I lost him."

Drake scraped the dirt back into the hole and replaced the sod.

We ran back toward my bike. A miracle we didn't twist anything considering both boys had us at a gallop in the dark. We were almost there when headlights illuminated the street.

We dove out of sight, thankful for the cover of a thick tree. Peeking around the bark, I noticed a computer screen inside the vehicle.

The police.

My breath hitched. Another vehicle pulled up, revealing the green decals along the side of the first, Mesa County Sheriff's office.

A warm hand landed on my shoulder, "Shh." Drake's breath was hot on my ear.

The SUV rolled to a stop at the open gate.

A door slammed.

"Evenin' Deputy." Grandpa?

The deputy stepped out of his vehicle and shined a light on Grandpa with one hand and rested his other on his firearm. My heart thundered against my ribcage.

"What are you doing in the cemetery at this time of night?" He barked.

"My granddaughter and a friend visited today and her bike couldn't make it back home. I clean forgot about it 'til now. I'd hate to lose all that money if it got stolen."

"You know where?"

"No, Sir. Against a tree, I suspect."

The officer said something official into his shoulder mic and closed his door. Grandpa came into view. He had a bit of a limp tonight. He always blamed it on arthritis in his hips. Sometimes it hurt worse than others. The two of them worked their way up the path.

We were further away from my bike than I thought.

Drake squeezed my shoulder and pulled me toward Grandpa's truck. His sneaking skills were off the chart. We creeped to the wooden split-rail fence and Drake guided me over it. He motioned to Josh and assisted Tressa over when they stopped at the fence. Josh stepped over and joined us by the bed of the pickup. I lifted the tarp Grandpa kept in the back to keep storms off the wooden bottom, and beckoned for everyone to climb in. They moved to make room for me, and I checked for exposed feet or hands.

Hopping in, I landed next to Tressa. She put her hand on my arm, fingers shaking.

"Whelp. I guess a slipped chain is good cause not to ride a bike home."

"Next time try to remember sooner." I heard a grunt. A tire landed near my knee. It rolled over and the handle traced my scalp. I bit my lip. A hand shifted the handle up a smidge so it didn't dig in.

"Yes, Sir. I'll do just that. Thank you for all you do. Have a safe night."

"G'night."

The driver's door creaked shut, and the engine roared to life. Grandpa backed up and turned around. We stopped once and then again, sitting forever. Probably the stop light. Grandpa sure took his time getting home.

The engine cut and I heard him close the garage door. The world soon inundated in blue, the bicycle moved. The tarp disappeared and the brightness made me blink.

Grandpa's face appeared, each wrinkle exaggerated his angry scowl, "Alright you lot. You've got some explaining to do."

Chapter 23

Grandpa marched us into the house. Josh took off his dress coat and loosened his tie. Drake left his mud-covered shoes by the kitchen sliding glass door. His face and pants were smudged, dirt embedded itself under his nails. I moved the blankets off the couch from watching the movie. Tressa and I sat down on it, while Josh took up residence in Grandpa's easy chair. Drake hung back, avoiding the only seat left next to me.

Grandpa put his hand on Drake's shoulder. He jumped and gripped Grandpa's wrist, giving him a menacing glare.

"Have a seat, Son." Grandpa's low and gentle voice a life preserver in the tension. He stood, steady as a rock while Drake processed through a range of emotions. Anger and fear morphed into shock. Neither moved. Drake's brow furrowed. Grandpa nodded toward the couch. I patted the spot next to me and Drake lowered himself down, ever vigilant to what Grandpa did next.

Grandpa dropped with a groan onto the coffee table. Dad had made it for Grandpa in Tech Ed a long time ago. I think Dad called it Shop Class. Placing his hands on his knees, he allowed his gaze travel to each of us. The clock click-clacked, the only sound beyond that of our breathing.

Grandpa started with Tressa, YOU OK?

FINE. SCARED. NEW. Tressa looked ready to go do it all again. She gave Grandpa a half smile.

I NEED YOU SAFE. I ENJOY YOU STAYING HERE AND HAVING FUN. BUT. I PROMISED YOUR MOM YOU STAY SAFE. YOU THINK MOM OR C-A-S-E WORKER OK WITH GETTING IN TROUBLE? YOU THINK THEY LET YOU COME BACK?

Tressa's face blanched. I put my hand over my mouth. We could've been in huge trouble tonight. Would Tressa be able to come back over? Did we get Grandpa into trouble?

Josh hung his head. I turned toward Drake, who narrowed his eyes at Grandpa as if trying to size him up.

I WANT VISIT AGAIN. A tear traced down Tressa's cheek.

ME TOO. Grandpa responded. ALWAYS WELCOME. PROMISE ME, NO MORE NIGHT TRIPS.

Tressa nodded, her bottom lip quivering. She launched herself off the couch and hugged him. Grandpa rocked her a little. She scooted back and he signed, GOOD GIRL.

Tressa returned to the couch and put her head on my shoulder. I had a feeling Grandpa would save me for last.

SORRY, Grandpa apologized. CAN'T SIGN AND TALK SAME TIME.

NO PROBLEM, she replied.

Grandpa's lips went flat and he arched a brow. Not last, next.

"Amie, what were you thinking?" Disappointment etched his face.

"I wasn't," I ducked my head, twisting my shirt in my hands. I hesitated to meet the storm brewing on his face. Why try to explain the war I had with myself about going? The jumble of emotions, the pressure of staying part of the group, not wanting to go, but doing it anyway.

"Look at me," Grandpa commanded. Drake's breathing hitched, he glared at Grandpa, fire rolled through his expression.

Grandpa and I locked gazes.

He had a way of reading people. We somehow could communicate across a table without speaking. Shame and guilt crept up my spine, but I didn't move. This was part of it. Grandpa tilted his chin, studying the ceiling.

"Mmhmm." He exhaled and studied me for a minute longer. "Next time, I expect you to not cave into peer pressure."

See, I'm an open book to him.

"Talk to me, Amie." He continued. "We're a team. I don't care how bad Tressa thinks she needs to go do something after dark. She wants to fit in so bad that she's willing to do dangerous stunts to do it. I need you to be that rock. You will do better, next time."

"Yes, sir." I moved from the couch and gave him a hug too.

"I love you, Scamp." Grandpa's breath tickled my ear. "If anything happened to you…"

"I love you too." He held my face in his hands and kissed my forehead.

"Why don't you take Tressa into the kitchen for a snack, while I speak with these two young men."

I waved to Tressa to follow and we went into the kitchen.

"Now. Joshua." I didn't want to hear the rest of what he had to say.

Nothing really sounded good to snack on. My stomach burned with the realization that we could've died at the cemetery tonight. We scared people off, but what if they chose to do something else? I almost got us killed. I let the scalding water purge the dirt, willing it to wash the guilt away too.

Tressa bumped my shoulder after I dried my hands. WHAT?

WE CLOSE DYING TONIGHT. I dragged the cookies out of the cupboard. BE CAREFUL NEXT TIME.

HOPE NO NEXT TIME. Tressa nibbled on a cookie with one hand and signed with the other.

SAME. I watched the den

Grandpa knew how to figure out the best and most effective punishment for any given circumstance. He'd give it to you and then move on. He expected maturity to come with learning from a mistake. I knew there'd be more checking in times and less freedom.

HOW MILK AND COOKIES P-U-N-I-S-H-M-E-N-T? She tilted her head waiting for an answer.

At the fridge I took down my "Visiting Auntie," note and threw it away. I set the gallon container of milk on the counter.

YOU FEEL HAPPY NOW?

NO. I SAD. MAKE GRANDPA SAD. Her chin dipped.

G-U-I-L-T. HE KNOWS WE KNOW. WE GO BED AFTERWARD. NO OUTSIDE TIME TOMORROW. WE TALK WITH YOUR MOM. NOT SAME FREEDOM.

Tressa set down the cookie. LIFE HARD.

AGREED.

I handed her a couple of glasses and she set them on the kitchen table.

"I'm sorry, Grandpa," Josh's voice caused me to tune back into the den. "I'll think about the consequences next time."

"Good." Grandpa's reply and their handshake sealed an unwritten contract. "Now go grab a working bicycle from the garage and bring your Jeep back from Duck Pond Park. No dawdling."

"Yes, sir." Josh stepped out of the den in one stride. He exhaled, rubbing at his chest. Determination sharpened his features and he left.

"Drake." Why did Grandpa choose him last?

Drake's stared at the couch arm, jaw clenched. I frowned. What did he expect Grandpa to do to him?

"Look at me, Son," Grandpa commanded.

Drake's eyes held fire and he grimaced.

"This is a safe place." Why wouldn't it be safe? It's always been a refuge to me.

Drake faltered, the fire dimming, replaced with confusion. His eyes traveled around and then his nose flared, chin held high when he resettled his gaze on Grandpa.

"I don't know you well. I'd like to change that, but I need to know what kind of man you anticipate becoming."

Drake blinked.

I translated for Tressa the best I knew how.

WOW. She signed. GRANDPA COOL. MAYBE HELP D-R-A-K-E BE NICE.

I nodded and continued.

"You have so much unused potential stored up inside of you that's going to waste. I know you're smart, protective, and have great ninja skills."

The light shined brighter in Drake's eyes. Grandpa had Drake's full attention. Grandpa did that. He spoke life into people and then held them accountable to reach their full capabilities. You wanted to change because Grandpa believed in you.

"Tell me about tonight." Grandpa leaned his elbows onto his knees, rubbing at the achy joint.

"Amie had given me," Drake paused, "Um."

"Pag's name?" Grandpa finished.

"Yeah." Drake winced. "I didn't want to tell my parents, so I used the Homecoming dance as my cover."

My chest loosened to hear that he'd gone alone. Tressa smirked at me. My face heated.

"Coach's door wasn't all the way locked and I used the computer in his office. I found there were two Pago… Pagi…Page…"

"That's why we called him Pags," Grandpa interjected.

"Oh. That makes sense." Drake leaned forward, excited to share. "There were two grave markers for the same guy. The same date of birth, but the death dates were farther apart."

Sadness sluiced over Drake's face, "But I didn't think about everyone else like you told Amie." His voice ended in a hoarse whisper and he stared at his feet.

"What about the rest?" Grandpa urged.

Drake's head snapped up, surprise laced his features. He cleared his throat and went on, "We discovered one grave in the Catholic section of the cemetery, and the other in the pauper's field. The craziness started when we got to the second. The records show it as the earlier grave. We scared someone off. I'm not sure how they didn't hear us sooner, because Josh scared Amie. That girl could scare the ectoplasm out of a ghost."

Tressa snorted after I translated that part. I shoved her shoulder. She laughed harder.

"They'd dug a hole, not big enough for a coffin, a box maybe, but… I don't know." Drake sighed. "The hole was empty, but it didn't look like they'd taken anything out. No depressions. And they used my shovel. I filled in the hole and we escaped back toward Amie's bike. That's when you and the cop showed up."

"I'm glad you all made it out safe. That coulda been dangerous."

Drake hung his head, "Yes, sir."

"Amie's intelligent. While she knows how to hold her own, she isn't as physically big as you and Josh. Now, like I told Josh, I need you to step into that protector role. It's not a job to take lightly."

Drake nodded.

"Good man." Grandpa patted his shoulder.

Drake lifted his chin. Admiration reflected in his eyes, lighting his face into a smile. Grandpa called the maturity out in him.

An engine slowed to a stop outside. The garage door banged. Josh must be back.

Grandpa moved to stand, but he struggled to get momentum. I moved to go help. Tressa grabbed my arm. WAIT.

Drake stood up, steadied his stance, and held his hand out. Grandpa clasped his forearm and Drake pulled him up.

Grandpa gave Drake a playful slap to his shoulder, "Thanks 007, think we should call it a night?"

"Yes, sir."

Tressa smiled at me, batting her eyes.

Before I could sign a snarky response, Josh stepped in and said, "Cookies," in his best Cookie Monster impersonation and grabbed two.

I held the plate out to Drake when he joined us. He took one.

Tressa signed, THANKS. Then she put her hands on her hips, waiting for him to repeat it. Baffled, Drake glanced my way.

"Thank you," I said and repeated the sign.

Drake flattened his hand and brought his fingers to his chin. He brought it down, like I did.

Tressa beamed.

Grandpa bowed deep. YOU'RE WELCOME.

"Gentleman," Grandpa looked at the guys, "it's time for you to be gettin' on home. Don't forget the shovel."

"It's already in the Jeep," Josh said around a mouth full of cookie. He gulped down a glass of milk in two seconds and held another cookie in his mouth to sign, GOOD NIGHT.

Drake turned at the door, "G'Night, Grandpa."

Grandpa waved at him. He locked the sliding door and turned to us. WHY BOTH STILL HERE? BED. SLEEP. NOW.

Chapter 24

“First you throw books at people, and now…” Mom paused, the video feed blinked. She worked at reigning in her emotions. “Now you sneak out of the house to go to the cemetery after dark.”

“That makes it sound really bad.” I winced, my shoulders drooping.

“It is bad, Amie.” Mom yelled, the speakers crackling. “To top it all off, you put a young deaf girl in danger.”

“But…” I started to say.

Mom cut me off by holding up her hand. “I don’t want to hear any excuses. This is horrible and embarrassing. I’m surprised you’re not calling me from the detention facility. Or the hospital or the police calling me saying someone kidnapped you or worse. Your knitting and crocheting privileges are gone until January 1st.”

“That’s two months. I just got them back.” What was I going to do?

"Whose fault is that?" I waited for the fiery energy from my mom to ignite my computer screen.

"But what about the dishcloths you wanted me to make for Christmas gifts?" Mom wanted everyone on the engine and dispatch to have one.

"That's what craft fairs are for." Mom raised both eyebrows, daring me to open my mouth. Wisdom sealed my lips. "We've been away for stretches of time before. Acting out in this manner, will not happen again."

Dad came on the screen. "And no cell phone until January 1st either, for back talking. Hand it to Grandpa, now."

I pulled out my cellphone and turned it off. Grandpa took it out of the room, to who knows where. Asking where he'd taken it would imply sneaking, which would add to my sentence. Not if I could help it.

"You can work with your group on your class project," Dad continued. "But you're not hanging out with them on personal time. Clear?"

"Yes," I winced. "What if we have to work on the project outside of class?"

The corners of Dad's mouth turned down, his eyes narrowed. "Then your grandfather will accompany you. We'll be home in a couple of weeks."

They ended the conversation and I stared at a blank screen.

I dragged myself to the couch to curl up. Grandpa cringed when he sat down next to me. He patted my leg. "I guess it's you and me now. Tressa said thanks for the weekend. Her foster mom is livid too. She came back early from her trip."

"Why the yarn?" I moaned.

Grandpa chuckled, "All actions have consequences, good ones and bad."

"On the outside it looks like I'm spiraling out of control, it doesn't always feel that way though."

"You've gotten into more trouble since starting this project," Grandpa had a point.

"Yeah. Now what?"

Grandpa nodded, "It's about time."

"What?" I turned to find a wide grin splitting his face.

"You haven't been in much trouble your whole school career. Might as well get it outta your system now. Your Dad and I spent half of his freshman year in the office."

"How can you be excited about this when you've been disappointed in me?"

"I still am. Growth doesn't happen on easy trails. It hurts that you couldn't come to me in person first. And it's going to get harder before it gets easier."

"How much harder?" I whined.

"You need to apologize to the deputy from the cemetery. I only guessed you piled into the truck. I didn't see you do it. The light in the garage helped me to discover you'd pulled it off."

Knots snaked their way into my gut. Grandpa's judgements turned out far crueler than getting my yarn removed. "I think you're worse than Mom in doling out punishment."

"Look on the bright side, you only have one night to dwell on it."

"That's comforting," my voice dripped with sarcasm.

Grandpa winked, "In the meantime, there's always chores."

Chapter 25

The high-pitched creak of the book cart didn't calm my nerves. Pushing it along the stacks didn't relax me this time. For a prisoner on death row, there was no comfort.

I wanted to go back to bed. Sleep escaped me the night before, worry gnawed on me. Maybe I'd be calling my mom from the detention facility after all.

Pierce came up from the other side, with a snarky smile plastered on his face. I opened my mouth to tell him off when the color drained from his skin. He left.

Odd.

"I found your note in my box, Amie." A deep baritone voice echoed in the empty library. It could only belong to one person.

"Deputy Will," I grimaced when I turned. Longest. Day. Ever.

"I spoke with Miss Phelps. She said we had the whole hour to talk. Why don't you grab your stuff in case you need to go to your next class when we finish?"

He stayed at the end of the row, and I dragged the complaining cart out toward the checkout desk. He flinched at the rotating squeak, "Sounds like I need to bring my WD-40 down from the office."

I shrugged.

Deputy Will stood an imposing six feet plus. His thick muscles bulged out from his short sleeves. He wore his hair in more of a military style. "Once a Marine, always a Marine, Amie." He told me at the last friends dinner. Mom showed me her yearbooks a couple of times, and he always ended up two pictures away from her. Deputy Will Brackett started out skinny as a stick and wore his hair in an Afro. His dark skin a beautiful contrast to Lucy's, his wife, peaches 'n' cream complexion. They made an amazing team. Lucy's pregnancy excited me to no end. My heart twisted. Could I get a baby blanket finished in time? Would my prison sentence be commuted?

One of the freshman girls walked by gawking at Deputy Will with stars in her eyes. I glanced back to make sure she hadn't turned into a puddle of drool. Deputy Will shook his head. He didn't miss a thing.

I collected my backpack and muttered a see-you-later to Monica, who stood there looking puzzled. The school gossip chain would be at it soon enough.

Exhaling, I found the hallway blissfully empty. Our footsteps echoed down the corridor. Our school stood just outside the posted city limits, which meant the school resource officers came from the sheriff's department or the district safety team.

"Your mom said you've been having a rough couple of weeks."

"They haven't been my best."

"How bad?" Deputy Will squinted.

"No yarn until the new year."

"Wow," he whistled. "At least there's only two months left."

"Yeah, I don't think I'll make it through Thanksgiving break."

Deputy Will's laugh loosened the worry settling into my shoulders. We walked past the front office to one, with a long window, the school resource officers used. A broad-shouldered man with sandy hair, polo shirt, blue jeans, and cowboy boots stood at the front desk waiting for his kid.

Deputy Will took a seat at a small side table and motioned me into the one across from him. "Your note said you needed to talk to me?"

"It's about some of that trouble. On Friday..." My hands fidgeted, missing my yarn. "And something else."

"I'm glad you want to talk to me about the cemetery. Why don't I take your mom off of hold and have Deputy Logan Reid join us?" They knew. Great. He leaned back and rapped a knuckle on the window, motioning to someone. Deputy Will then pushed a button on the round conference phone sitting on the table.

"Hi, Mom." I sighed.

"Amie," her voice came out flat.

"I was trying…" I stammered.

"I told you to take care of this." I imagined her tapping her foot and drilling holes into the wall with her eyes. "First thing in the morning..."

"None of the resource officers were here, Mom, I had to go to class."

"No excuses, young lady, I'm tired of hearing them." I threw my hands up.

"Cecilia," Deputy Will broke in. "We had something to handle this morning, and I didn't make it to the high school until an hour ago."

Thank you, I mouthed.

Deputy Logan came in, jaw clenched, green eyes blazing. So he wasn't waiting for his kid after all. Scrunching down in the chair didn't help the height difference. From my seat, he towered over me. He didn't sit but crossed his arms over his thick chest.

My heart bounced a crazy rhythm off my rib cage. Swallowing hard, I craned my neck up. Curiosity popped out, "Did you see us at the cemetery?"

"No," Deputy Logan growled.

"Cool," I put my hand over my mouth, hanging out with Tressa rubbed off on me.

"Amie," Mom scolded, "apologize now."

My face heated up. Mom treated me like I was a kindergartener.

I let out a breath, "The note I left asked Deputy Will to help me find you. Looks like it worked." My voice shook and my insides turned to butter. My mouth watered and lunch threatened to come up. I peeked around to find the trash can about ten feet away. I'd have to go through Deputy Logan to get to it. Never mind.

"Amie, I expect an apology." Mom snapped.

"Cecilia, give her a minute," Deputy Will cocked an eyebrow at me. Everyone's patience ran thin.

Straightening, I found Deputy Logan had followed my gaze to the garbage. The corner of his mouth twitched. He sat down in the chair in front of him. Now he had a direct view to the back of my soul. Fantastic.

I rubbed my sweaty palms on my pant legs. "I'm sorry we…I deceived you. I'm sorry you had to come in on your off hours to talk with me. I hope you're able to get enough rest before your next shift. And I'll answer any questions you ask."

A fleeting glimpse of surprise crossed his face. It left me wondering if I'd imagined it. His eyes narrowed in a new level of scrutiny.

"Good," Mom's curt reply made me jump.

"You're in a lot of trouble, young lady. Illegal removal of a corpse will get you jail time." Deputy Logan's voice held an edge.

My mouth opened and closed. This must be what a fish out of water felt like. The shaking started at my feet and worked its way up. I shrank back. Jail. I really stepped into it good this time. Did I doom the rest of the team?

"Amie," Mom shrieked, "You did what?"

"Ma'am," Deputy Logan never moved his laser focus off me. "I want to hear it from your daughter."

"The…the hole wasn't big enough for a body, only a box. And we didn't remove anything, we filled it back in." I bit my lip and picked at a loose fiber on my pants. A lump formed in my throat. "But I have no way to prove it."

"I'm listening," Deputy Logan hadn't moved.

Stick to the short version. "Paglione has two graves. Crazy, I know. That's why we had to investigate."

"After hours?" Deputy Logan challenged.

"I didn't say we were smart." My eyes widened. Oops. I couldn't read his expression. I winced and continued, "One's in Calvary and the other in the pauper's field. We found the actual one just fine. But when we got to the other section, we heard two people. We heard a guy's voice for sure, but I don't know about the other. They took off when we came. We found Drake's shovel in the hole, and it was empty, I swear. Drake filled it in and took his shovel with him."

"No body?"

"No, sir." I sighed. Life as a felon, that changed everything.

"I believe you." Deputy Logan bounced his knee a couple of times like Dad did after a long shift.

"You do? Why?" My head swiveled toward Deputy Will, who pointed back at Deputy Logan.

"Two sets of footprints going one way and three coming and going from the bike." Deputy Logan continued, "Why only three, I thought there were four in your group?"

My ears burned, "Tressa's deaf and the darkness doesn't combine well with communication. Josh gave her a piggyback ride."

Silence invaded the room, which didn't help the tension. Deputy Logan peered out into the office for a minute. "I don't think your grandfather knew you were in the truck at first since I placed the bike in the back. It landed softer than it should've. Unless I find out otherwise later, I'm going to leave it as a citation for trespass."

"Thank you, Deputy." Mom regained her composure and spoke in her official voice.

"Ma'am, who's going to sign the citation?" Deputy Logan asked the air.

"I can help with that."

My insides shattered and I shrieked. I had to grip the back of the chair to keep from twirling out of it. Grandpa stood behind me, adjusting the hearing aid I sent whistling from my screech.

Grandpa chuckled, "I guess it is a might tense in here. Drake's right though, you'd scare a banshee. Why those two graveyard ghosts didn't run off before that, I'll never know."

Deputy Logan cracked a smile and reached for a metal clipboard in front of Deputy Will. How long had that been sitting there? He handed it to Grandpa and stood next to him to explain it all. Grandpa signed it.

"Stay out of trouble, young lady." Deputy Logan gave me a stern look and Deputy Will walked with him to the main office area. "This is why I don't do kids, Will. My ear is still ringing."

Deputy Will laughed, "You did great. I thought you liked scaring people."

"She nearly puked all over my boots. I just bought these." The closing door muffled the rest. Grandpa sat in the seat Deputy Logan vacated.

"Your mom said you're paying her back for the fine." Grandpa showed me the citation. "She and I went over options before the school called her."

I gasped, "There goes my book money for about four months, or more."

"Now, Amie," Deputy Will came back in. "What's the other thing?"

"Monica and I found a letter in the library from Pierce. We think his mom's beating him. He comes in every once in a while with part of his face a little swollen."

"We can make sure Child Protective Services checks it out."

"I don't necessarily like him, he's really annoying. But no one deserves to be abused either." I traced the edge of the table with my fingernail. "Pierce and Drake almost hate each other. Do you think Pierce followed the guys to the cemetery?"

"Time and investigation will tell." Deputy Will scratched his chin, "Pierce, is he the kid with the skunk hair who took off when I walked up?"

"Yeah."

"I'll keep an eye on him."

Chapter 26

No one spoke a word in history. Tressa watched all of us at once. We'd grouped up for the last 20 minutes of class.

"Remember, time is running out, and the competition is right before Winter Break." Mrs. McCreedy finished and the noise level elevated, not by much this time.

Everyone looked away when my gaze roamed the room. We were the talk of the school today. People were gossiping, planning, or trying to look busy to avoid doing the project altogether.

Tressa patted the table twice. COP TALK WITH ME WHEN MOM DROP ME OFF.

Kathleen voiced for the others, mostly Drake, who didn't attempt to sign.

"They pulled me out of second hour," Josh added.

"I missed lunch," Drake's stomach protested the absence of food.

"No library aid for me," I paused. "Did you get a citation for trespass?"

Everyone nodded.

"Well, well, well," Pierce towered over Tressa. She shrank down and frowned. "If it isn't our favorite jailbirds."

"Pierce," Mrs. McCreedy called, "Please go back to your group to work."

"Get lost," Drake snarled at Pierce.

"Enjoy life on the outside while you still can," he sneered.

"Pierce, it's best if you leave," I chimed in.

"Aw, poor babies," Pierce whined.

Josh grabbed Drake's arm, but he yanked it out of Josh's grasp. He stood up, face flushed, and a vein throbbed at the side of his neck.

"Come on guys. Walk away," I pleaded.

Pierce and Drake stood toe to toe, stiff and unwavering. Josh moved forward to help, but Tressa grabbed his shirt. He frowned at her, but she shook her head. Josh let out a breath and settled back in his chair, the scowl never leaving his face.

I heard Pierce came in punk rocker makeup this morning. The principal made him clean it off, but the black still shadowed his eyes. One looked a puffier than the other.

"Drake, let it go." My right hand rested on his left arm. His muscles were taunt. We locked eyes. A storm brewed deep inside his irises. Anger, confusion, hurt.

"Gentlemen, return to your seats," Mrs. McCreedy commanded.

I gave Drake an affirming nod and tugged on his arm. Confusion still reigned, but he took a small step back toward our group.

"Aw, how cute Amie, you trained the monkey to listen."

A steel expression replaced the confusion on Drake's face. His arm shot out of my hand. Drake's fist thudded on Pierce's jaw.

Pierce dropped to the floor and didn't move.

Drake sat on top of his desk. He winced and rubbed his rib cage.

I sighed and put my hand on his shoulder. His head moved and spine stiffed, but he didn't brush my hand off.

Mrs. McCreedy pointed a finger at Drake and yelled, "You stay there."

She kneeled next to Pierce, "Pierce, can you hear me?"

Students crowded. Didn't he need more air than that? "Take a step back."

No one moved.

"Go sit down," Josh bellowed. Our classmates drifted back to their groups, craning their necks to see.

"Pierce?" Mrs. McCreedy shook his shoulder. His chest rose and fell in a steady rhythm. She rubbed a knuckle on his sternum, he groaned.

Deputy Will marched in with Mrs. Carlyle, the school nurse, on his heels. Kathleen followed them in, I didn't remember her leaving.

Pierce sat up and shook his head. His gaze roamed around the room.

"It's history class, Pierce." He looked at me, then Drake. His eyes focusing on the shoulder my hand rested on. His eyes narrowed.

"Can you stand, Pierce?" Mrs. Carlyle asked.

He stood, giving Drake an icy stare. He allowed Mrs. Carlyle and Kathleen to guide him out.

Deputy Will hovered near me. He motioned me out of the way. I moved. Drake looked over when I released his shoulder. He saw Deputy Will and stood. Deputy Will latched onto Drake's elbow. Drake flinched and fisted his shirt near his rib cage.

Why did that hurt?

Deputy Will gave me a puzzled look. I shrugged.

Drake turned in my direction, pain shadowing his face.

"I quit," he rasped.

Chapter 27

NO. NEED FINISH. Tressa waved at Drake. He rotated away from her and let Deputy Will lead him out of the class. Students muttered to each other.

Drake quit.

Sinking to a chair, I put my head on my arms. What were we going to do now? Josh sat in numb silence, his jaw hanging open as if his best friend just left.

I found Mrs. McCreedy over by her desk. She pinched the bridge of her nose, staying that way for at least a minute. She glanced at the clock and straightened. "I'd like everyone to take out a piece of paper. Write your name, the date, and the time. In a paragraph, describe what you witnessed in class today in case our school resource officer needs it for his records. Be as detailed as possible. Turn them into the class box when you're finished."

Pencils scratched across paper. I stopped and wondered about Tressa.

WHAT, she shrugged.

YOU FEEL PENCILS ON PAPER?

Tressa looked around. NO, BUT FEEL TENSION.

"Oh," I mouthed and bent over my paper to finish.

❖❖❖

Tressa and I jostled our way through the crowded hallway on our way out of school.

WHAT NOW? NO D-R-A-K-E?

I DON'T KNOW. YOU HAVE IDEAS? I pointed at her.

NO. BUT NO SKUNK FACE.

She made me laugh. SAME.

Tressa slowed at the office and we both stared at the open door. After a minute, I glanced out the front glass doors and saw Tressa's foster mom pull up to the curb.

MOM HERE.

THANKS. TELL ME HOW GOES. Tressa almost knows me better than I do.

OK.

SEE YOU LATER. Tressa's hand rocked an L, moving it downward. Waving, she bounded through the school entrance.

I crossed the now familiar threshold to the office and took a seat along the padded bench opposite the long counter separating the secretaries from the students. Drake talked with Deputy Will. More like listened to a lecture. Drake stared straight ahead without blinking.

From my spot, I observed Mrs. Carlyle examining Pierce. An angry purple and red bruise outlined his jaw. Two paramedics ignored me on their way by to the nurse's office. Before long they came back out taking Pierce with them.

Mrs. Carlyle eased down next to me, "Can I help you, Amie?"

"I'm okay, thank you."

"Why'd you come to the office? From what I understand, you weren't part of the problem."

I opened my mouth to answer, but nothing came out. Why did I come? Both Tressa and I knew I'd do it.

"I suspect," Mrs. Carlyle grinned. "That someone could really use a friend right now."

"Suppose so." I stared down at my shoes.

"Good friends are hard to find." She patted my shoulder and returned to her work area.

Drake's parents materialized, and I watched the color drain from his face. His mom slammed the door. He was the only one who didn't jump. The whole family filed out a short time later. Deputy Will crossed his thick arms over his chest and frowned. Drake saw me for the first time since I entered. He paused at the door, sending me an uncertain gaze. His dad pulled him out of the room.

"What's up, Amie?" Deputy Will spoke but continued to watch Drake and his family.

"I dunno know." My shoes needed a cleaning. My chest tightened, a lump in my throat made breathing weird.

"You've had a rough couple of days."

"Guess so." I bit my lip.

"You want to talk about it?"

I lifted a shoulder.

"I'm here when you're ready."

"Sure." Hustling out of the door, I stopped to think. Did I walk home today? Did Grandpa say he'd come and get me? My lead-lined shoes caused my feet to drag. Sitting on the short, ornate wall, I pulled my knees up to my chin. I removed Grandpa's picture from my backpack and stared at it.

The picture blurred.

"Wow. That's a picture of my grandpa. Nice." Joe Billings' granddaughter, Mona, took up residence next to me on the wall.

"My grandpa," I whispered, pointing him out.

"Pags was weird." We both said it at the same time and giggled.

I stifled a sob. The tears streamed down my cheeks. I leaned my head on her shoulder and I felt the pressure of her cheek on the top of my hair. She wrapped me in a hug. Trying to suppress the emotional storm only made it worse.

"I heard about what happened in class." Mona rocked me.

"I tried to…to…stop it. But it…it…it happened anyway." My stomach ached from crying. "Now…now…Drake quit and…and…don't know what to do."

"Maybe you don't have to do anything."

"Huh?" I looked up at her, the tears slowing. She produced a package of tissues. I sat up to blow my nose. How could one nose produce so much snot?

"You're not responsible for anyone but you, ya know. Drake made his choice, and his reaction isn't your fault."

Glancing down, I'd frayed a whole tissue all over my pants.

"You should take up knitting or something to keep your fingers busy."

"I can't until January 1st," I hiccupped.

"Ohhh." Mona's almond-shaped eyes widened.

"Yeah." I winced. "Pags had two graves, and we trespassed at the cemetery after dark."

"That would do it." She paused. "How does someone have two graves?"

"One's empty."

"How…" I could see the gears turning in her expression. Her crimped hair had a bright pink streak in it.

"We're researching the uranium boom for the history project in Mrs. McCreedy's class."

"I'm in her AM class and my group is researching the Storm King Fire from 1994."

"Wow. That one killed 14, right?" I squinted, trying to remember the details.

"Yeah, not many people know it by name." She high fived me.

"My parents are wildland firefighters."

"No way, can I interview them?"

"They're out of town right now with a hotshot crew."

"That's too bad," she sighed.

"Mona, are you okay honey?" A Japanese woman in a neon pink shirt and yoga pants walked up.

"I'm fine, Mom." Mona stared into my eyes. "We're both gonna to be alright."

"Amie?" Grandpa followed close behind Mona's mom.

"Thanks, Mona," I whispered and waved at Grandpa.

"Anytime."

"You want to hang out?" I regretted it as soon as it popped out.

"What's wrong?" Mona's eyebrows knitted together.

"I can't have friends over right now."

She waved it away, "There's always lunch."

"Mrs. Billings. I haven't seen your family since the funeral. How are you?" Grandpa exclaimed as realization dawned.

"Ed. You should come to dinner soon," Mona's mom beamed.

“That’d be wonderful,” Grandpa watched us approach. “Our girls are turning into beautiful women.”

“I’m a hot mess.” I grunted.

“There’s beauty in that too,” Mona hugged my neck and we parted ways.

Grandpa dipped his head toward the school. Deputy Will disappeared into through the glass doors.

Chapter 28

"And neither one has been at school all week?" Grandpa slid a plate of his fabulous breakfast eggs under my nose.

"No," I closed my eyes, savoring the way they melted in my mouth. "Rumor has it that they're suspended for a couple of weeks. Pierce has a concussion, so he won't be back for a little bit, anyway."

"It sounds like this rumor is a little more accurate this time." He added butter to his toast and took a seat.

"Yep," I reached for the honey and added it to my golden bread. A neighbor up our street gave it to us from his own beehives.

"You think Drake will be at the BMX races today?" Grandpa raised his eyebrows, uncertainty gracing his face.

"I hope so." I gulped my milk.

"What do you hope to accomplish by going? He quit the group and I doubt he'll change his mind." Hot coffee steamed his glasses when he took a swig and returned the cup to the table.

"I'm not going to try and talk him back into the group. I think Drake needs a friend," I paused. "Something hurt him in class when Deputy Will tugged at his elbow. It wasn't an emotional hurt. He looked like he'd let out a big secret."

"And why hide a bike injury?" Grandpa scratched at his chin.

"Exactly," I leaned forward. "Does this mean you'll take me?"

"I think you got your curious streak from me."

"Yes." I pumped my fist.

"When does it start?"

"Practice is at one and the race starts right after."

❖❖❖

The county fairgrounds had the rodeo arena along with a couple of other arenas under pole barn roofs, stables, the BMX track, and a little league park. Grandpa and I edged our way through the bleachers near the finish line and sat down. The early December breeze still held a breath of autumn air, which would change after the first snowfall. But I determined to enjoy it while it lasted.

An older woman plopped a tote, cooler bag, and bleacher seat next to me in a huff. Her silvery hair fell into her face and she brushed it over her shoulder. She stared at Grandpa far longer than I expected. Rotating, I found

Grandpa fixated on a hill along the track, his back ramrod straight.

My new neighbor noticed me for the first time, "Haven't seen y'all here before."

I returned her sweet smile, "It's our first time."

"Who're ya here ta see?" She adjusted the seat to hook underneath the bleacher and hold it in place.

"Drake." My water bottle clacked when I flipped the top, Grandpa remained still as a petrified tree.

"Ah." She sighed. "His people don't come to watch. He's a nice young man though, a little on the quiet side. My grandson said the racin' makes him feel free. It's 'bout time he found a girlfriend."

Gagging, water dribbled down my chin. "We aren't...he's not...We're in the same class."

Grandpa chuckled and patted my back.

"Mmmhmm." She leaned around me and winked at Grandpa, who cleared his throat.

The racers lined up their bikes at the starting line. My eyes traveled along the row, looking for a familiar face. I glimpsed black hair with a white streak down the middle. "Pierce?"

The lady sniffed. "He's an odd one. Hasn't been racin' long."

"I wonder why?" I mumbled. Pierce said he liked to skateboard, so why BMX? If he's so hurt, why's he here?

"He and Drake seem to be rivals." The lady crooned, "Maybe they're contending for your heart."

I groaned. Grandpa didn't even try to hide the grin.

Chapter 29

BMX Track Starting Line

The soreness in his ribcage added to his pounding head. With any luck, the adrenaline would ease the pain off for a little while. Getting close to people proved tricky. The forced break from school, refreshing in one way, tried his endurance with the incessant stream of criticism from his mom.

Still. She did allow him to race. Told him to come back refocused and ready to do better. Even if it required lining up with the enemy.

Letting out a breath he released the frustration out past the starting line. Gazing down from the rise, he visualized each turn. He scratched the top of his head before donning his helmet, fastening the chin strap. A familiar bike tire came into view on his left. Each race, the same conversation.

"My grandma came to watch me today. She's sitting over there." The kid pointed toward the bleachers.

He fulfilled his obligation and followed the direction to the seating area. The person sitting next to Grandma piqued his interest.

"Amie? What's she doing here?"

"Is that the girl next to Grandma?"

He didn't mean to say it out loud, "I think so."

He watched Amie spew her drink. Thankful no one sat in front of them. A warm sensation spread through his chest. He'd never experienced anything like it before. It didn't hurt. In fact, the empty ache filled in and the soreness eased.

"You okay?" the kid pointed at his chest.

"Yeah, why?" He looked down to find he'd gripped the front of his racing jersey. He released it and concentrated on the upcoming sprint down the track.

"Riders! Ready!" The gatekeeper called.

Leaning on the gate, it dropped. He careened down the track, around the turns, and flew over the hills. It hadn't been his most spectacular run, but the first time he had an audience. One that cheered him on.

If having a friend felt like this, he'd protect it.

Chapter 30

Amie

"Now what do we do?" Josh asked. This was our first meeting since the blow up. "Our project is due in a few short weeks. Competition is right before break."

I DON'T KNOW, I managed to speak and sign together. I put my head in my hands.

Three knocks on the table brought my focus to Tressa's smiling face. She pointed to me. YOU READ. J-O-S-H TYPE, ME CREATE.

CREATE WHAT? Josh's signing improved.

Tressa opened a folder and pulled out a piece of paper. On it was a diagram of a rotating mining belt with spots to hold information on.

G-E-N-I-U-S. I told her.

WOW, Josh added.

Tressa beamed.

MY FAVORITE IDEA, Josh put his hand on Tressa's. Then drew it away. MOVE WITH HAND OR M-O-T-O-R?

HAND. Tressa motioned as if she turned the crank.

GOOD IDEA, I pointed to the rule book. CAN'T HAVE CONTINUOUS M-O-T-O-R.

I SEE. Tressa's smile couldn't be bigger.

BUT, I made sure they were watching me, WE MUST LEARN INFORMATION TOGETHER.

OK, Tressa shrugged.

WHAT WE KNOW NOW? Josh lifted his hands.

U-R-A-N-I-U-M DANGEROUS. BOOM. Tressa's eyes twinkled.

We all laughed.

TWO GRAVES, Tressa pointed to my pen. I started writing.

ONE EMPTY. Josh signed.

GRANDPA AND JOE NOT LIKE P-A-G-S. I caught Kathleen's smile out of the corner of my eye. She told me how proud of us she'd become as we worked to learn ASL.

WHO JOE GRANDPA? Tressa squinted, trying to remember.

M-O-N-A.

SMALL MINES TROUBLE FOR MONEY. Josh's face twisted into a frown and he froze.

I UNDERSTAND, Tressa patted his arm. I added to the paper, “money troubles that the smaller mines had with the bigger companies.”

After a long minute with no one adding anything new, Tressa finished, NEED READ MORE.

❖❖❖

For the first time, we had a definite goal. Lunches became our extra meeting times. We had too much to do and not enough time to do it in.

Walking up the driveway, I did a double take at the top of the porch stairs. A manila envelope rested in the corner near the stairs under the front window. I approached it as if a bomb would go off. Nothing happened when I tapped it with my toe. My name was on the front. Pinching one corner, as if it were a dead rat, I carried it inside.

Letting it rest on the kitchen table, I used a knife to pry open the flap. Nothing poofed out, but I saw a small stack of papers. Sliding them out of the envelope caused them to fan out on the surface. A note was at the top of the pile.

Dear Amie,

I know I quit the group. I won’t be back to school until after the break. I couldn’t let some of my research go to waste.

Drake

I flipped through the papers.

No way.

The fair grounds were once called Uranium Downs and, it used to have a dog and horse racing track.

Cool.

Chapter 31

Conversations buzzed in the cafeteria. Tressa set her tray down with a thud and sat down next to Josh. His cheeks turned rosy. They started talking about how the morning's classes went.

I dug into my lunchbox for my sandwich. Mona and Monica took up residence at our table too, Monica wore her hair up in two buns that reminded me of teddy bear ears. Her light brown shirt and dark brown skinny jeans helped intensify the persona.

Mona wore a red, Asian style button-up shirt. Her eyes sparkled while watching Josh and Tressa. "Are they together yet?"

"Maybe." I grinned back.

I SAW THAT, Tressa's mock anger dissolved into a nutty smile.

I introduced Monica and Mona to Tressa. They both waved.

HOW KEEP APART? M-O-N-I-C-A, M-O-N-A. CLOSE SAME. Tressa shrugged.

"Our names are similar." Mona replied after I explained.

"Never thought about that, we've always been in different classes. Maybe that's why." Monica tapped her cheek, thinking.

Josh translated for Tressa. She pointed to Monica and made two fists above her head like Monica's buns and twisted them. Tressa then pointed to Mona and made an M circle her face.

"Uh," Mona leaned back, "What's all that?"

"Monica's name sign is for the ears she's always wearing or putting her hair into. Yours is an M and the other part is beautiful."

"Aw!" Mona said and signed, THANK YOU.

Tressa clapped her hands once, NOW WORK.

I exaggerated rolling my eyes. Tressa scowled but then dissolved into giggles.

Five minutes later I had everyone caught up on the manila envelope Drake left me.

I KNEW D-R-A-K-E NOT QUIT. Tressa high fived Josh.

"Grandpa said they had a Miss Uranium contest, and the grand prize winner collected one ton of uranium," Mona twirled her finger near her temple in the sign for crazy.

Tressa laughed so hard I thought she'd fall off the chair.

"People used to use the uranium mill tailings, the junk rock dirt stuff, as foundation filler on houses. Many of them had to be gutted and redone or the family had to move. Realtors are required to test flower beds and other rocks to make sure they aren't radioactive." The table fell silent. We all stared slack jawed at Monica.

"What?" Monica gave a sarcastic frown. "I have grandparents too. I don't only read Manga, ya know."

SMART, Tressa answered.

"All of this is really good. Now all we have to do is find these things to cite and write it up." Josh kept signing while we talked.

"Maybe we can do a couple of interviews," I added.

YES. THAT. Tressa pointed to me.

"I can ask Mom if we have any of Grandpa's old stuff," Mona paused to text her mom. "Amie, do you think your dad will loan us any fire gear? Unless he has it all with him."

"If not, I'll call around to some of the others."

"Thanks!"

"You can video chat with my grandparents," Monica perked up. "They both live out of state."

Josh volunteered, TRESSA, ME, VIDEO WITH, and then he used Monica's name sign.

Monica flashed a smile and held two thumbs up.

Chapter 32

The book cart glided noiselessly through the aisles. Deputy Will made good on his promise to spray it with the WD-40. Looking both ways down a book aisle, I half expected Pierce or Drake to materialize. Both seemed to dwell in the library more, before they got into trouble.

An adult came through the doors, disrupting my train of thought. I could tell by how Monica greeted them. Her voice carried, but the other person's sounded muffled. I'm sure I'd find out soon enough.

Both of the boys acted tough, but were they hiding behind their masks of fear? Monica and I suspected Pierce had an abuser, but we had no proof beyond the letter. Oh no, I forgot to give it to anyone. Drake hid his fair share of aches and pains, but he also rode a BMX bicycle. But what if both of them were mistreated by someone close? Drake's face lost all of its color when his parents came in the other day. Mine would too if Mom and Dad showed up to school after I punched someone's lights out.

"What if?" I mumbled.

"What if what?" A man spoke behind me.

"Argh!" I jumped, releasing the books in my hand.

Thump.

Turning in a slow circle, I found Deputy Will holding one book above his head, while the other one lay splayed open at his feet.

I sighed. Could this school year get any worse?

Putting my wrists together in front of me, I responded to his raised eyebrow, "How much time do I get for assault?"

"Flying books and you don't get along. I need to remember to call you out of whatever zone you're in before I approach next time. A warning will do, for now." He picked up the book from the floor, checked its spine label. Deputy Will moved a couple of tomes apart on the shelf and slid the book into place. "What d'ya say?"

I let out the breath I held. "That'd be nice."

"Besides," Deputy Will nodded. "The books didn't even touch me, my hands are too fast." He chose a book off of the cart, scanned the label and the shelves before handing it to me. "This one's closer to where you're standing."

Fitting it in place, I moved down the row and gave him a another one to put in place. "You didn't come all the way down here just to help me shelve books, did ya?"

"And if I did?" He studied the stacks and motioned his thumb further down the row.

"It seems silly. Not that I mind." I added, trying to save myself from the awkward. It didn't work. "But not everyone has the patience for it."

"True." He paused and glanced my way. "I don't have the patience to do this every day like you do. Today I'll make an exception if you'll chat with me and answer some questions."

We rounded the corner of the next corridor of books. "Um. Okay." I gulped.

"I noticed when I brought Drake into the office that you looked like you wanted to talk to me, but you weren't sure. Then, you and Mona cried, after that, y'all got picked up. Just now, I saw the gears in your head spinning so much you didn't hear my approach. What's up?"

"What if I tell you something that turns out to be false? Or, what if I tell you something and it gets an innocent person in more trouble? What if it turns out to be nothing at all and I think it is something? But isn't?" I bit my lip.

"What if you let me decide?"

The next book in my hand stalled on its way to be replaced. What if . . .

"I don't have any proof." The non-existent whisper hung in the air.

"But something doesn't feel right, correct?" Deputy Will grabbed a set of three books.

I nodded.

"Who?"

"Both." I squeaked.

He raised an eyebrow, "Pierce and Drake?"

"Uh, huh." I went for the last book

"Okay, what is it?" He snagged it before I did and cracked a smile.

"Abuse," the word strangled my throat. I put my hand over my mouth and waited for Deputy Will's reaction.

His smile drifted away. He stilled the book an inch above the shelf, then slid into its proper place. "What kind?"

"Physical, I think." The dam that held it all in for weeks exploded. "Pierce's jaw was swollen before Drake nailed him. Drake hid the fact he was in pain and looked like he wanted to disappear when his parents came. Then there's the note, and Drake quitting the group but not quitting the research. He's still helping mind you, but can't officially at school, I don't know why he has to deliver it in a manila envelope when we aren't at home. Now both guys could be in unsafe places because they're stuck at home. But what if it's because they both play in edgy sports with injuries?"

A weight lifted.

Deputy Will smirked, "You've been holding that in for too long."

"But now, what if me not saying anything sooner causes them more pain and they die?" I threw my hands up. On the way down, my knuckle slammed into the cart handle.

Ouch.

I shook my hand and cradled it with the other one.

"Amie," Deputy Will rested his hands on his tack belt. "Stop borrowing trouble. We're talking now. We can do something now. Right?"

I shrugged. The knots in my stomach coiled tighter.

"Besides, you told me once about Pierce, remember?"

"Not Drake though." I whined, not letting myself off the hook that easy.

"You still have the note?"

On our way to return the cart to the counter, I added, "Thanks for fixing the wheels."

"Anytime."

Monica began the process of filling it back up. Yanking the note out of my backpack in the clean sandwich bag I put it in, I handed it across the counter to Deputy Will.

"Mind if I keep this?" He asked, scanning the paper.

"I don't want it back."

Monica bounced up and down. "Do you need our fingerprints for comparison?"

"Probably not, Monica." Deputy Will deflated Monica's balloon. She stopped jumping, her lower lip jutted out, and her shoulders slumped.

"Remember when out parents filled out that missing child paperwork in like second grade?" I bumped her elbow.

Monica sprang back up. "So, you already have me on file? Cool."

I snorted, and Deputy Will swallowed a sudden smile. He shook his head as he made his exit from the library.

Monica squeezed the oxygen out of me, "Wait'll we tell Mona."

Chapter 33

“Please, Mom?” We were on video chat. The sun coming through the tent made colors shimmer across Mom’s face. The air mattress she sat on protested her movement. On a fire, tents were sometimes a luxury. The staging area was far enough away for the crew to camp out.

Dad appeared on the screen. Soot smudged several places on his cheeks and chin. A forehead ring announced where his hard hat stopped on his brow. He looked like Grandpa, the way the grime and dirt filled in his pores. He rubbed a hand down his face and grimaced at what he found on his palm. Dad retrieved his shower bag from next to Mom. Ash streaked the top of the sleeping bag when he stood, “What’s so important?”

“Mona and her mom invited Grandpa and I over for dinner tomorrow. It’s not a school night. She’s Joe Billings’ granddaughter and it’s for the school project.” Dad scrutinized the screen. “I know I’m grounded for all of eternity, but can’t we go? Grandpa will be there.”

Mom and Dad stared at each other. Her shift would start soon. Dad gave his I-don't-have-a-problem-with-it shrug.

"That'll be fine," Mom concluded.

"Whoohoo!"

❖❖❖

Grandpa parked the truck in the garage. "That was an excellent meal."

"Mona scanned a whole bunch of photos for us to use on our display. This project will take us to the state level." I beat Grandpa to the sliding door at the back of the house.

Tripping on the threshold, I rammed into a kitchen chair. My shoulders tensed. My heart picked up in rhythm. Something felt wrong. But what?

The kitchen faded to a memory of Mom and Dad when they went out on a date before they left. She wore a black tunic dress with leggings. Dad took her out to one of the fancier restaurants in town. He donned a three-piece gray suit and brown dress shoes. Dad winked and promised not to break curfew. The world righted itself to the present.

I flipped on the light.

Nothing stirred in the kitchen. The den was how I left it. A blanket strewn over the couch. I did a double take of the refrigerator. Mom's favorite magnet twisted at a diagonal. She always liked it being straight up and down. I've been corrected on it so many times, I turn it the right way any time I bump it. My arm knocked it sideways before we left for dinner with Mona and her mom.

I fixed it too.

An invisible vacuum sucked the oxygen out of my lungs.

Grandpa slid the glass door shut and I heard the lock click into place. He stopped humming, "The perfume you're wearing reminds me of the stuff your Ma wears on date nights. Something's a little different about it though. Can't put my finger on it."

Grandpa saw the magnet on the fridge, "You hit that thing again?"

"Grandpa," I squeaked. "I'm not wearing any perfume."

The leathery skin of his hand gripped my wrist. Holding me firm, Grandpa yanked at the locks of the back door. He hustled me into the garage. He eased the overhanging door down and picked up the extension phone on his work bench. Grandpa dialed a number. "I think someone broke in or is still in my house."

Chapter 34

Light shone from every window of the house and then some. There were at least four deputies and two state troopers clearing the home. I'm not sure why so many decided to show up, but they cleared the garage first.

The cold metal of the truck's tailgate bit into my skin, making my rear go numb. I drew up my knees and wrapped my arms around them before allowing my chin to rest on my boney knobs. An unmarked vehicle pulled into the driveway, and another deputy exited. Grandpa met him halfway. I heard snatches of questions about how we knew it was a home invasion. The scene blurred, and the backs of my eyes burned. I quit staunching the tears and let them run. No one would notice me in the dark shadows of the garage.

Someone had been inside our house. First the tire, and now this? Why? Why not ransack the place? Was it meant to go unnoticed? Did they plant listening devices? Hidden cameras? Why spy on us? We don't own anything important.

Mom's strong and tough, but I'm not. I want to be tough like she is. The tears flow hot and salty down my face. Anger churned in my chest at the stolen peace. How could I sleep here tonight? Why do I always turn into a soppy wet mess? All I seem to do is cry. Some tough girl I'm turning out to be. My jeans soak up the waterworks, while I buried my face in my knees.

The truck bed shifted. Grandpa must be finished talking. I'm grateful he doesn't say anything. Instead, he bumped my arm. I take the offered travel pack of tissues.

"Thanks." Unfolding into a cross-legged position, I blew my nose. It's loud, as usual. Grandpa always accused me of being related to a goose whenever this happened. "Don't call me a goose, Grandpa."

"That's a first. I've never been called Grandpa before."

I expected to see Grandpa's jeans, instead I saw olive drab pants with a stripe down the side and a black tactical boot swung back and forth from under the tailgate. Both of my hands trapped my nose in the tissue. I looked left and found Deputy Logan focused on Grandpa's conversation. My whole-body heated up starting with my toes. Maybe he didn't notice. Yeah right.

I finished clearing my nose and ducked my head, "Sorry."

A chuckle rumbled deep in his chest. "You give your statement yet?"

"Twice."

"Are there any older siblings that could've pulled a prank?"

"Nope. I'm it." Without realizing it, I'd shredded another tissue all over my lap. I brushed the pieces onto the truck bed. "Not knitting is killing me."

"Does it keep you from mincing tissues?"

"I said that out loud?" Rubbing my temples didn't hide the bewildered look that crossed Deputy Logan's face. "I'm not allowed to pick up a stitch until after January first. I'd rather have my phone taken away. Oh wait. It was."

"What horrible thing did you do for that to happen?"

I frowned at him. "My friends and I waltzed through the cemetery after normal hours and narrowly avoided being eaten by ghosts and members of the undead, only to escape by sneaking past the guard at the gate, and duck into a transport vehicle leaving the premises."

Deputy Logan coughed, "Wow." It sounded more like he choked on spit, but we'll go with surprise. "You always have this much imagination?"

"Doesn't everyone?"

"No." He scrutinized my face. I remembered him telling Deputy Will he wasn't cut out to handle kids.

"Thanks for coming so fast. I thought it'd take at least 10 minutes to get here or more. You made it in three."

He let out a breath. “I was in the vicinity.”

“Making sure we stayed out of the cemetery?” The conversation from earlier distracted me from thinking about the house for a little bit. Calm settled around my shoulders.

“Maybe.”

“If the other people weren’t at the cemetery” — my voice dripped with sarcasm — “They were probably in my house.”

They were in my house!

I gasped. My head snapped up. Deputy Logan’s leg stilled. Grandpa and the other law enforcement officer turned our way.

I vaulted off the truck, raced down the driveway, and cut around the corner to the front porch. The enclosure offered more seclusion, away from prying eyes.

I tucked myself next to the stairs at the corner of the walled in porch. A tall bush stood in front of the mid-level wall, which made for a great place to hide. The rough wood bit into my back.

A hummingbird took up residence in my chest where my heart was supposed to be. My hands quivered like aspen leaves on a tree. Air going to my lungs in short supply.

“Amie!” Grandpa’s shout crackled between fear and frustration.

Boots clomped along the sidewalk. They were too quick for Grandpa’s stride.

"I see a shoe." It may have been Deputy Logan, too much blood whooshed through my ears for me to hear much of anything else. The bottom step creaked and the man himself appeared. Checking on me, he rotated away to scan the area and left me to the solitude.

"Amie," Grandpa shook his head as he ascended the stairs. He eased himself into the swing at the end of the porch and set it in motion. Silence reigned.

About the time my heart set itself into a gentle pulse, Deputy Logan said, "They cleared the house, so you can go to the den area if you'd like to go back inside."

Grandpa moaned out of the swing and stopped next to me to offer me a hand. "We'll be safe inside."

Staring at his gnarled hand, I hesitated. "What if . . . What if it isn't?"

"What if we catch a cold waiting for everything to be finished? Or what if killer mosquitos swarmed the yard and we don't have bug spray?"

"Very funny, Grandpa." It didn't help. Banging my head on the porch wall, I rubbed it and looked up.

"What if we offered our guests some bottled water?"

Nodding, I rose to my feet. Grandpa held out his elbow and I slipped my shaking hands into the crook of his arm. Forcing myself to not peek back, I let Grandpa lead me inside.

Taped to the underneath side of the deck railing was another manila envelope.

Chapter 35

One eyelid cracked open when Grandpa dropped a pan in the sink. I lifted my head off the couch in the den. The sun danced through the back door.

"Sorry, Kiddo." Grandpa called. "My arthritis is acting up today. Must be a storm coming."

I stumbled into the kitchen and banged my knee against the counter. Again? My gaze drifted to the top of the fridge. How long would the new cookie jar have gone unnoticed? When Grandpa asked about it, deputies discovered a hidden camera inside. They found a second one in the upstairs hallway light fixture. My stomach knotted. Where there more?

Grandpa slid a cup of coffee in my direction. The warm, syrupy liquid woke up my brain. I tugged at the crumpled shirt I wore, and I tried working out the pillow crease in my face. A knock sounded at the back door. Josh stood peering in through the glass. Grandpa motioned him in.

A chortle escaped from Josh, and his eyes refused to move from my hair. He turned his cellphone screen toward me. The back half of my hair tried reaching for the ceiling, the left frizzed, and the right looked stringy.

"What are you doing here?" I yawned. My puffy eyes were gritty.

Josh held a device under my nose, "Grandpa asked me to search the house for any more bugs or electronic devices they may have missed last night."

"Mmm hmm." I took another sip of coffee.

Turning, Josh followed his blinking box through the kitchen and into the den. How had he not hit a wall yet? He disappeared up the stairs, ghost-walking our house in his preoccupied trance with the screen.

"That kid," Grandpa shook his head, "He's as absentminded as they come when he works with his gadgets."

Josh reappeared and set my hairbrush next to me on the counter before exiting the front door. I pulled a stool from under the counter and sat down. Do I feel mad at him for walking through my rooms or grateful for the assistance?

Not awake enough to decide, I yanked at the tangles in my hair. The hair tie on my wrist soon captured my ponytail in place.

Josh re-entered the house through the back door. "I can't find any other cameras except the one we installed on your truck, Grandpa."

Accepting a cup of coffee, Josh gagged on the liquid. He reached for the sugar on the counter and scooped a spoonful in. Grandpa offered the cream and I grinned at him, letting the steam from my cup curl around my face.

"You okay?" Josh tilted his head.

I lifted a shoulder, "No one last night denied the possibility of it being related to the cemetery stuff."

"That's scary."

"Josh, do you have a little time? I need to go to the hardware store. Would you stay here with Amie while I'm gone?"

"No problem, Grandpa." Josh stood taller.

"I should be back in thirty minutes." He disappeared out the back.

"We can start assembling our project on Monday. Drake's research got us going." Josh drummed his fingers on the counter.

"Oh, Drake." I swiveled off my perch and strode to the front door. Josh followed me out to the porch. Kneeling, I gripped the manila envelope and yanked it. The tape snapped and snarled in protest.

Taking it in, I cut a thin strip from the top. Josh peered in and nodded his approval. I upended the contents. A prepaid cellphone, charger and note skittered onto the counter.

Josh unfolded the paper. "It's easier to talk this way, Drake. P.S. It's fully charged."

I bit my lip and stared at the phone on the table. My own uranium bomb. “I’m not supposed to have a phone right now.”

“You want me to take it when I go? There’s no obligation to talk to him. He did quit.” Josh stated a fact, but he seemed uncertain about not talking with Drake. He tapped at the phone and then met my eyes.

“Would you talk with him if you took it with you?”

Josh shook his head. “No, I’ve been texting him our homework assignments. We almost take all the same classes. I wouldn’t need it to speak with him.”

Drake. The phone. Trust. Not knitting for the rest of my life. What if I could help figure out what was going on? What if I couldn’t?

“What if he’s in trouble, Josh?”

“Drake is trouble. I like him too.”

“I don’t like him like that.” I lunged at him.

“Yet.” Josh smirked and dodged my punch, sloshing his coffee.

Music sounded from the mobile and the screen flashed on. My stomach tightened.

What am I doing?

Me: Hi

Drake: Took you a minute to find this.

Me: Someone broke into my house last night.

Drake: Scary. U ok?

Me: I think so.

Drake: What was stolen?

Me: Nothing. They planted cameras.

Drake: What!!!!

Me: We found them all.

Drake: Whew

No new info on the research.

Me: We are building on Monday. It's ok. You good?

Drake: Bored.

"Well, we can change that." Josh grabbed the phone.

Josh: Hey bro. Josh. On a scale of 1-10, how much do you

"Josh," I yelled. One of us had hit the send button in the struggle.

Drake: ????

Me: Ignore the last message.

Drake: Can Josh bring me the art project packet?

"Here." I slid the phone back. Josh gave me his best cheeseburger grin. I peered over his shoulder.

Josh: No prob. Where you want to meet?

Drake: Uranium Downs, BMX Track.

Josh: See ya. Grandpa's back.

I rushed the phone up to my room and hid it under my mattress. Grandpa's truck rumbled into the driveway.

Josh tapped his fingers on the table. "Why won't Drake's parents get his homework? It's starting to sound like school holds him together."

"I told Deputy Will that I was worried." I slumped back into my seat.

"Too bad Drake couldn't come stay with my family for a while. He'd be safe." Josh rolled his eyes. "Well, as long as you don't count harassment from my sisters."

I'd learned at lunch one day that Josh's four younger sisters were two sets of twins. "You could use an extra guy at your house."

Josh half smiled. Grandpa closed the garage door.

"What'd I say wrong?" My stomach lurched.

"It's not your fault. There's supposed to be another boy." Josh fidgeted with the coffee cup handle. "I'm a twin, too. Someone stole him from the hospital right as we were released."

Chapter 36

Tressa waved Josh and I over to her desk in history class on Monday. An upside-down box covered the top of it. Josh lifted the edge to peek underneath. Tressa popped the box and caught the tip of his nose.

He jumped back and rubbed it. WHY NOT SHOW LUNCH?

FORGOT. MOM BRING. Tressa did a happy dance. Rubbing her hands together, she stretched out her hands, wiggled her fingers, and lifted the box revealing a conveyor belt with yellow clumps of papier-mache attached to it for our uranium rocks. She moved the belt with a hand crank on one end and the whole assembly rotated. Tressa pointed both fingers at the corners of her mouth and pointed them up and out at the same time. PAH!

WOW. I answered and gave her a high five.

"What's that sign mean?" Josh asked Kathleen.

"It is the same sign as finally, but it's used for Ta-Da." Tressa's interpreter patted his shoulder.

“Oh.” Josh pointed to the mining belt, COOL.

Tressa hopped up and down.

Mrs. McCreedy came over to inspect Tressa’s hard work. She touched Tressa’s shoulder. GOOD JOB.

THANK YOU.

I think Mrs. McCreedy gave Tressa the world.

“Time to settle in everyone.” Mrs. McCreedy waited for us to focus on her. “We’re working on projects for the remainder of the week as regionals are this Saturday in our gym. All projects will need to be ready by then for judging. Several other districts, including the other middle and high schools in the valley, are competing as well. This weekend will determine who goes to State in the spring.”

Miss Perfect groaned, “But that’s the beginning of our break.”

“You and your parents have known about it since August. Every team needs to be represented this weekend. Get to work.”

Josh pulled out paper and scissors. He began cutting out the information for Tressa to glue to cardstock and then attach it to the exhibit.

I unfolded my school issued laptop and found the files we had on our citations and annotations. Each source required an explanation of what we learned from it and how we used it in our project.

Tressa nudged me. PICTURE FOR DRAKE.

GOOD IDEA. I ASK. We'd let Tressa in on our undercover texting with Drake at lunch. I stretched the kink out of my back and made my way over to Mrs. McCreedy who typed on her computer.

"What can I help you with, Amie?" She finished and swiveled her chair to face me.

I fished the cell phone Drake gave me out of my pocket. "Could we take some pictures on my cell phone of our project and send them to Drake? Can we do that now or do we need to wait until class is over?"

"I'll allow it today, but this is the only time. Clear?" She checked for understanding.

"Yes, Ma'am. Thank you."

I took a couple of what Tressa built and the information on it. Josh took a group selfie around the project since his arms were longer. Turning the computer screen to show the cover page, I'd put Drake's name on top.

PERFECT. Tressa nodded her approval.

Josh gave two thumbs up. I added the cover page picture to the others and sent them all to Drake.

"Clean up your areas," Mrs. McCreedy called out. Glancing at my watch, we had three minutes left in our day.

Performers picked up fabric pieces. Several wrestlers slid their tri-fold boards into the slot between a bookshelf and counter. Monica's team put everything in a box and packed their school bags. She wore a reddish-brown stocking cap with fox ears, a black top, and red plaid pants.

Tressa guided our project into its box. Not leaving all of our hard work to chance, she refused earlier the offer to leave it at school. Monica glided over and poked her nose in the box.

"Wow," she mouthed to Tressa.

THANK YOU, Tressa answered. They bumped knuckles.

"Bye, Miss Kathleen," Josh and I said together. Tressa's interpreter waved and exited the class right before the bell.

CAN I CARRY FOR YOU? Josh pointed to the project.

Pink tinged Tressa's cheeks. She bit her lower lip before nodding.

Josh picked up the box and cleared his throat before exhaling. He held his elbow toward Tressa. She frowned and glanced my way.

I shrugged my backpack on, and Monica slipped her hand into the crook of my right arm. Monica's eyes disappeared with how big her smile stretched across her face.

SAME, I signed with my left hand.

REALLY? Tressa's eyes widened and she swallowed.

She eased her left hand around his elbow. Josh relaxed his arm against his side, and they exited the classroom.

"That is so adorable." Monica released my arm and squeezed my neck.

"Ack," I choked, "Breathing is good."

"Oh, yeah. Sorry." Monica re-linked elbows and dragged me out of the room.

We settled into the flow of students in a mass exodus from the building.

"So romantic," Monica sighed.

"What's romantic?" Mona joined our chain to my left. She wore a navy-blue business suit with her hair in a bun. I was in the middle in my t-shirt and jeans feeling very underdressed.

"Nice outfit," I complemented.

"Thanks, I'm the prosecutor for mock trial."

"Josh likes Tressa, and he offered her his elbow to walk out of class today," Monica explained. We somehow shifted to walking in step.

"Why not his hand?" Mona wrinkled her nose and frowned. "I know he's a gentleman, but I didn't think he was that old-fashioned. Even if it is cute."

"He's carrying our project out to Tressa's car," I explained.

"Gotcha." Realization dawned on Mona's face.

"Amie. Monica. Do you have a minute?" Deputy Will stood outside the library entrance. We angled toward him, the others moving around us. "Mona, how are you?"

"Fine, thank you." Mona gave my arm a yank. I stumbled into her and Monica slammed into me. The drama teacher walked by. A large piece of plywood obscured everything but his fingertips, the top of his balding head, and his green Converse shoes.

"Sorry, whoever that was," he called.

"It's okay," Monica yelled back and giggled. "He never seems to see where he's going."

Mona pushed me upright, Monica hadn't moved back, and I ended up becoming an Amie sandwich.

"What can we do for you today, Deputy Will," I grunted. He chuckled.

"Did either of you put the letter you gave me in your mouths?" Deputy Will rested his forearm on his tack belt.

"Ew. How unsanitary." Mona pretended to puke.

"Yuck," Monica shivered and held her tongue out gagging.

"Gross." I winced and shook my head.

Deputy Will cleared his throat, the grin growing bigger. Where we really that funny? "Thanks ladies, have a good rest of your day." We watched Deputy Will walk away. He scratched his head.

"Hmm." Mona frowned. "I wonder what that means."

"There were only two guys in the library that could've left the letter, Pierce and Drake. I don't know which book it was in or this would be easier." I chewed on my lip. "The prints may not be in the system or they wouldn't ask about a corner being bitten. DNA?"

"Remember our conversation the last time we talked about the missing person's database?" Mona looked at

Monica. "They only have descriptions and fingerprints, Anime Girl. But let me know if you find out anything different."

"Oh." Monica slouched, then perked up. "You make me sound like a library superhero. I like it."

"Good. Because you are one. Both of you." Mona jiggled my arm.

Me? A superhero? Superheroes are supposed to fix problems, not create chaos. I tilted my head and gave Mona a sideways glance.

Mona nudged my ribs with her elbow. "Really. I'm serious."

Most of the students had drained out of the building. The three of us remained linked together as we headed for the front exit. Mona checked to see if the coast was clear of adults, and we skipped the rest of the way out.

Chapter 37

"Grandpa, can we get the Christmas stuff out of the attic before Mom and Dad make it home?" I tossed my bag on the couch in the den. It was Thursday. T-minus 42 hours to the competition and counting. I needed something to calm the butterflies that were twitching around the inside of my ribcage.

"Why not? They should be home this weekend in time to see your project." Grandpa's voice floated down from the bedrooms.

Walking upstairs to the hallway, I grabbed an old broom handle with a hook on the end out of the closet. I reached up, caught the eye of the screw in the ceiling and pulled down so the attic ladder could descend. I hoped the burglars, or whoever they were, thought it was a plant hanger.

I surveyed the area behind me. No one was there.

The folding ladder was on an antigravity release. Sort of. Dad installed hydraulics, like the kind on car trunks or back windows, so it wouldn't slap anyone in the face. After the second time it happened, Dad had enough. I scurried up and looked around for the Christmas stuff.

It ended up buried under all of Grandpa's uranium memories. Oops.

I slid the half-empty box away from the others so I could get to the random assortment of containers with holiday cheer peeking out. Turning to see if I moved everything, I jammed my elbow into the corner of a metal box.

"Why is it called a funny bone, when it hurts?" I fell to my knees, sucking in air.

Grandpa's head popped up through the attic floor. "Because your humerus is the upper arm bone that connects the radius and ulna. Plus, it isn't me who's in pain, it's you." His eyes twinkled, but he didn't laugh.

Grunting, I stood and wheezed out, "Thanks for the science lesson." Turning my arm to inspect my elbow, I found a two-inch scrap that started collecting blood. "Good thing I'm caught up on my shots."

Grandpa's laugh echoed off the rafters, "Come on down and we'll give your elbow CPR."

I rolled my eyes. My elbow throbbed reminding me it was still alive. "First aid?"

"That too."

"I'm not going down empty-handed though." Setting the container next to the other uranium things, I dragged the first box to go down toward the ladder.

One gauze-wrapped arm later, because regular band aids were impossible to find in my house when we needed them — and ten trips on the ladder later — the guest room looked like a Christmas rummage sale. After supper we put up the tree and followed that with hanging lights, holly vines, and bows on the stair railing. Grandpa let me shimmy up the ladder to hang snowflakes and garland from the ceiling and around the lights.

I put the ladder back in the garage, locked it, and headed back into the house. At the bottom step, Grandpa appeared at the sliding glass door and upended an empty box on my head. It smelled of cinnamon and musty ribbon.

"Gotcha good that time, Scamp," Grandpa hooted, releasing me from my cardboard prison.

A tickle made my nose twitch, and I pinched it. I examined my arms — glitter covered every square inch — I swiped at it but there was enough sweat on my arms to hold in place. I sneezed. The world shimmered and sparkled around me. I couldn't fault Christmas for being glittery.

Chapter 38

This was it. Our last class period to finalize and strategize our projects for the next day. Tomorrow was the epic showdown and win, lose, or draw —we'd survive the day. Our exhibit was sure to make the finals for state competition in Denver.

Mona must have picked up the firefighting gear Dad said she could borrow. It no longer rested by Mrs. McCreedy's desk where I left it.

I sat in my usual seat next to Tressa, her eyes fixated on my hair. Pushing her shoulder, I shrugged at her.

She held up a pointer finger, YOU. She balled her other hand into a fist, T-I-N-K-E-R-B-E-L-L. And proceeded to punch the pointer finger.

Huffing, I slumped in my chair with my arms crossed.

Josh dropped into the chair on my right, "What'd you do? Get in a fight with Tinkerbell? I think you lost."

Rolling my eyes, the sound of a high five behind my back drew Mrs. McCreedy's attention.

EMPTY CHRISTMAS BOX, GRANDPA, and pantomimed him toppling it on my head. My teammates burst out laughing.

Tressa stopped long enough to sign, SPARKLE.

Uh oh. This was how name signs were given. My wide eyes locked onto her's and I snapped the NO close to her nose.

YES. FOREVER.

"Argh," Defeated, I shifted to face the front of the class.

"Amie," Mrs. McCreedy smirked. "Wendy called from the office and wants her pixie dust back. But no worries, if you feel the need to start floating, I have a length of rope we can tie off to the desk to keep you attached to the ground."

Tressa pointed at me and roared after watching Kathleen translate.

Mrs. McCreedy signed, TIME CALM DOWN and turned to the class. "This is the last day for working on projects and getting them one hundred percent ready to go. I expect you to turn in your process papers and annotations online before class ends."

Whispered tension rippled through the room. The procrastinators in the class hunched over computers and projects with worry etched on their faces. The staccato of keyboard keys almost made me giggle. Turning on my own computer, the air grew hot around me when Josh and

Tressa leaned in to watch my screen. They both helped me edit our documents.

I FOUND NEW INFORMATION, Josh stopped me from sending in the document. We had fifteen minutes left in class. He gulped when I glared at him. Tressa shoved my shoulder and shook her head. Josh sent a silent plea for help Kathleen's way.

She nodded and motioned to Tressa that she'd take over.

He continued, "I contacted the university library about anything they had on uranium. Did you know they have a fair collection of stuff?"

"Josh," I snarled, "We are running out of time."

"Okay, okay. They are one of few places who have a complete set of *Atomic Age* publications. She let me look at some of them electronically. In one of the editions, it talks about how there was a group of international students who toured the area."

"What does this have to do with what we already have?" My brain was thinking of how much we'd have to do in twelve minutes.

Josh shrugged.

SHOWS EVERYONE WANTED COME HERE. Tressa raised her eyebrows in challenge.

A much needed cool clue. What if . . . ? I didn't have time for that.

WE CAN ADD ONE MORE? I put my hands in the shape of a square and then turned my hand like I was turning our project.

Tressa tapped her finger at her temple. YES. ROOM FOR ONE MORE.

Citing the source and adding the annotation to our bibliography had me sweating. Josh helped by showing me the information from his phone. The clock yelled we had three minutes.

Tressa pushed my face back to the laptop screen. FOCUS.

I made sure it saved and went into the file and made sure it shared with Mrs. McCreedy in the appropriate place. The saving wheel spun. No. No. No. I checked my internet connection and then it acknowledged the save.

I let out a long sigh.

GOOD. Tressa patted my back.

PEREFECT, Josh added, the bell ended the school day.

WE COME YOUR HOME TONIGHT AND FINISH LAST ONE? Tressa waited for my answer.

I lifted both shoulders. I HAVE ASK LATER. ENOUGH TROUBLE NOW.

They snickered.

FUNNY FRIENDS, I told Kathleen.

HAVE GOOD TIME TONIGHT. SEE YOU TOMORROW FOR CONTEST. Kathleen left for the day.

Josh tapped at his cell phone and he put it to his ear. "Hey Grandpa, it's Josh. Amie's too busy to ask, but can the group come over and finish up the project for tomorrow? We have one more piece of information to add. Uh huh. Thanks. Bye."

AND…? Tressa hurried Josh on by bouncing. I pushed my laptop into my backpack and wiped off our desks.

IF PARENTS SAY YES.

Tressa pumped the air. HURRY CALL, CALL, CALL.

Chapter 39

Undisclosed Location

Swallowing fire every time he inhaled made him wonder if she'd cracked a rib. He shivered in a ball on the cold kitchen floor. Her footsteps vibrated behind him.

How much longer would she let him live? Was it better to give up? On her liability list, his time could be now. What would Amie think if he died? The tile his elbow cracked on his way to the floor, now pinched his cheek.

His burner phone went off in his pocket. He forgot to silence it. Reaching for it, she slapped his hand out of the way and ripped his back pocket, extracting the device.

"Tsk-Tsk-Tsk," she clucked. "Aw, Drake. You've been texting our prize behind our backs. How delightful. I didn't even know it. Good job." Mom patted his sore head. "Amie says Josh and Tressa are at her house putting the last pieces of the project together. And you're invited. How cute."

"Why don't we join them, Dear?" Dad's voice sent shivers down Drake's spine. "We know the way there after all. It's a shame they found the cameras."

"You were the ones who broke in?" Drake ground out through clenched teeth.

"And slashed the tire. That one hurt me. It's a nice truck." The warmth from Dad's knee near his back made Drake hitch his breath.

"Excellent," Mom typed and spoke. "Be there soon."

"No," Drake hissed. "You leave them alone."

Hot pain-spiked tendrils radiated up his arm and down his side when Dad wrenched his wrists behind his back. A thin rope wound around his wrists, and the knot jerked him into Dad's knee.

"Stay down," Dad warned.

Drake moved to sit up, but Mom put her shoe into his gut. Colors and dots danced shadows in front of his vision.

"Come along, Darling," she crooned. "We either get answers tonight and find it. Or leave no witnesses."

The door slammed to the garage, followed minutes later by a motor turning over.

Drake coughed, tasting the copper. His tongue hurt where he bit it. The floor tiles came back into focus. Amie, Grandpa, Josh, and Tressa's lives depended on him now. Images of the cemetery at night flashed in his brain. Each of their names carved in a different headstone.

His parents were going to have to walk over his dead body before he'd let that happen.

A volcano erupted in Drake's chest. Heat swirled around in his torso and spread out to his limbs. The determination and frustration began evaporating the pain. With a concentrated effort he sat up. He drove his heel into the cracked tile. A shard popped out. He went to work breaking the bindings.

Chapter 40

Amie

"Excellent?" I frowned at the message on the burner phone from Drake. Grandpa found out about it at supper. Surprised, he allowed me to keep it. Grandpa said we'd discuss it later.

Tressa wrinkled her nose. NOT SOUND LIKE D-R-A-K-E.

BAD. Josh paced the length of the den and moved the curtain to check outside. The sun had disappeared over the horizon, leaving everything in shadow. GRANDPA TRUCK ON STREET.

Grandpa left to help one of the older ladies four houses down the road. Her sink backed up again, and Grandpa explained he'd be back soon. Josh returned with Grandpa's favorite Louisville Slugger, the one he hung on the wall. Tressa's eyes opened wide.

NO WORRY, Josh pointed to his chest. LITTLE LEAGUE CHAMPION.

I stretched an arm over the coffee table. Tressa took the last placard and attached it to our final information rock on our uranium belt. Our project looked great. A win tomorrow for sure.

CELEBRATE WITH COOKIES, Tressa pumped her fists in the air.

I LIKE HOW YOU THINK, Josh tossed the bat in the air and caught it.

We all trailed into the kitchen. Electricity skittered down the nerves in my arms and across my stomach. Eating sweets no longer sounded good. Josh ate one in a single bite, and Tressa picked two. His second cookie fell to the floor as the front door cracked and flew open to bang against the wall. Two people tramped in, dressed in black, guns raised. The front door rattled shut and they slid the chain lock into place. Josh hit the shorter one in the hip sending the gun sailing toward the back door.

Tressa shrieked.

The other man focused on us, slipped on the cookie. He regained his balance in time for Josh to hit him full force in the gut with the bat. Their momentum carried them into the den. The coffee table exploded beneath their combined weight.

They grappled together.

Grabbing Tressa's hand, we dodged the doubled over intruder, and ran up the stairs. The attic ladder took its merry time letting down. Tressa hopped from foot to foot. I pushed her up it and yanked it closed.

Moving Tressa back, we huddled under the table, hiding behind empty Christmas boxes. Tressa fingers glided over her cell phone, her face ghoulish in the screen light. My brain turned on.

What did I just do? I'd trapped us up here with no way out.

A shot rang out. Tressa grabbed my arm when I told her.

Josh. Tears welled up in my eyes.

They'd come this way in minutes. My breathing hitched. Moving over, I met something sharp with my arm.

A screwdriver.

Crawling to the hatch, I set to unscrewing the ladder from the hydraulic bolts. I shook so hard it took both hands to hold it. The end jumped out with every attempt.

"Come on, come on," I urged. Blowing out air, I tried again.

Success.

With both sides finished, I crept back to Tressa. She shoved her phone in my face and I saw an ongoing conversation with emergency dispatch. Tressa flipped it back to herself and answered the next question.

Muffled shouting snapped my head toward the ladder. It was only a matter of time . . .

Tressa tapped my shoulder. In the light of her screen she signed, I STAY. YOU RUN.

NO. TOGETHER, I answered. Hot tears dripped off my chin.

DARK OUTSIDE NOW. I QUIET, TALK COPS.

A scratch vibrated across the attic.

I put my fingers to my lips. Tressa texted something, and then turned off her screen. She moved another box to hide herself. I slipped over to the side of the ladder. They needed to see me first. I had to get them out of the house. But how? And where?

The cemetery. Deputy Logan.

A weapon. After a quick scan of the area and I came back with Grandpa's metal box. There'd only be one chance. Exhaling, I waited.

Light spewed from the hatch. It eased down. I needed it to go faster. Slamming the box down on the ladder sent it dropping at warp speed. Gravity carried the first rung straight into the shorter invader's face, followed by the box to the forehead.

I shot down the hatch and headed for our cracked front door. The bigger man caught me around the waist at the bottom of the landing. My banshee scream made him grimace. He growled when I poked his eye.

Thunk.

I dropped to the ground and the man grabbed the back of his head. A baseball rolled by me.

"Go," Josh rasped. He held a second baseball in his hand.

Throwing the chain off, I tripped out the door. And ran. My footsteps ricocheted back like gunshots on the quiet road. My lungs burned, but I didn't dare stop. After running forever, the four-lane intersection loomed ahead, and I charged forward. Tires squealed and someone yelled, but my pounding heart drowned out what they said.

"Please be there," I gasped.

Vaulting a fence proved harder than it looked in the movies. I bent in the middle and fell over it. Getting up, I dodged head stones and paused next to a marble bench. Someone tackled me. We rolled over the bench and I ended up with the smaller intruder sitting on my chest. My arms pinned under their knees.

"Help!" I screamed, thrashing. One wild kick landed in the middle of their back.

"How dare you," a lady's voice hot on my face. "Where is it?"

She shook me. "Where's what?" I yelled back. My teeth slammed together and I bit my lip.

My eyes adjusted in time to see her lift a fist.

"No!" The shout to the left of us made her hesitate. A blur shoved her off to the side. I cringed at the bone crunching thud. My heaving breath punctuated the stillness.

"Amie, you okay?" He wheezed gripping his side.

"Drake?"

"Yeah." He guided me to my feet, and we started away from her. "I didn't send that last text."

"Oh, good. I didn't think so." I wiped my lip. "It all happened so fast."

Drake pivoted, checking the area. We walked under a tree. He started to limp. "Where's everyone else? They okay?"

The wail of sirens broke the eerie quiet. I faced Drake, putting both hands on my cheeks. My throat constricted, "I don't know."

Someone let out a war whoop. Drake glanced behind him, fear rippled across his face. He lunged, wrapping me in a hug. My foot caught the corner of a headstone. A semi-truck like force hit Drake from behind, launching us into the grass between the headstones. The wind rushed out of me and I coughed. The man from the house leaned over Drake. He beat a steady rhythm on Drake's back, with his knee ground into my shin. Air filled the vacuum of my lungs and I wailed.

Blue and red lights flashed in crazy patterns off the trees and headstones. The man stopped thrashing his fury into Drake and twisted in the police's direction, his foot ground into my leg when his weight shifted. He rose to his feet. A flash from the cruisers glinted off metal in the man's hand.

"Gun. Gun. Gun." I shrieked.

Drake exhaled and his head lolled resting heavily on my shoulder. A rock dug into my shoulder blade.

"Wake up," I urged.

He didn't move.

"Don't die," I whispered.

Shots rang out and bullet casings fell hot on my ankle. The man's boot scuffed against my shoe. He moved forward. My fingers managed to find the pulse in Drake's neck. His heartbeat felt steady. What if I moved him and fractured something else?

Both sides shouted. More gunfire. Someone landed hard on the grass.

"Suspect down!" Several people called out.

I heard boots, swishing grass, and a couple of curses.

Light blinded me, "Amie?"

"Yeah?" I croaked. Someone kneeled beside my head. I saw spots and an outline. Others hovered over us, examining Drake.

"It's Logan, Amie. Are you hurt?"

"Yes. No. I don't know." I expected tears this time, none came. My breathing hiccupped. "I knew you'd show up."

He grunted, "That makes one of us. I hadn't planned on coming this way at all tonight."

"I'm glad you did."

More figures joined in, and my vision cleared. I wanted to wiggle out of the way, but no one seemed eager for me to move.

Deputy Logan bent closer to my face. "They're checking your friend for spinal injuries before we move him. Hang in there."

"He won't wake up," I wheezed. Drake's body pressed down making breathing hard.

"Heart rate — 120, respiration — 40, BP — 180/90," a woman's voice explained.

"Ready to rotate him onto the board?" another asked.

"Yep. We'll pack him out on this board to the gurney, there's no easy way around all of this."

An incoming siren paused and the extra lights adding to the chaos.

Deputy Logan moved to give the paramedic at my head more room. I could feel two more at my feet and side. They moved his neck enough to put a C-Collar on him. Someone counted down. Everyone lifted and rolled Drake onto a backboard. I sat up, feeling the cold void. My teeth chattered together, and goosebumps raced down my arms. My coat hung in the closet at home.

More paramedics rushed up to assist with getting Drake to the ambulance. One lady EMT turned my way and picked up her blood pressure cuff. I jumped when a blanket draped around my shoulders. Deputy Logan nodded to the woman when she stooped next to me.

My brain clouded over, everything slowed down. The cuff squeezed my arm. Can I sleep now? When did my thoughts sound so loud?

“Amie? Amie?” My head swung toward Deputy Logan. I blinked. He arched a brow at me. “Can you tell me what happened?”

“Tressa and Josh . . . My house . . .” I heard myself whisper. Life snapped back into focus. “They need help at my house.”

Jumping up to unsteady feet, my head woozy, I turned to leave the cemetery.

“Hey.” Logan’s hand on my shoulder stopped me. “Will’s with them and they’ll meet us at the hospital.”

“And Grandpa?” Velcro ripped and the blanket enveloped me in warmth again. Drake was halfway to the ambulance.

“Worried, but fine.” Deputy Logan tilted his chin toward my paramedic, and she guided me along the same path Drake took.

Two reflective blankets covered the attackers from head to toe. Dead. My steps faltered, slowing.

“Let’s not dwell on that right now, Hon,” she pointed out a headstone we needed to avoid. “You’re safe.”

At the ambulance, they transferred Drake onto a gurney and hoisted him into the back. The EMT steered me to the side door. Another EMT extended his hand down to me and assisted me up the stairs.

“We have a chair just for you.” He deposited me in a rear-facing seat and spooled out the seat belt so I could buckle myself in. The back doors closed. He crouched next to me, concern shrouding his dark eyes, his hair in cornrows. “What’s your name?”

“Is Drake going to die?” I croaked, my chin quivered, and I bit my lip to make it stop. Pain from the previous injury made me stop.

The vehicle lurched, but no one noticed. IVs and oxygen lines hung at various angles, paramedics moved around the bed on wheels, ignoring the jumble.

“Not if we can help it,” A blue gloved hand waved my attention back to my attendant. “My name’s Jamar Billings. What’s yours?”

“Amie Coleman.”

“Hi Amie,” Jamar held up his hand. I gave him a high five and knuckles when he changed his hand into a fist. A smile twitched at the edges of my mouth.

“Can you tell me what day it is?” Jamar asked.

“Friday, unless it changed to Saturday.” I frowned, looking for a clock. Gasping, my eyes widened. “Saturday is the competition.”

Jamar chuckled. “Let’s take care of the two of you first and worry about championship games later. Hmm?”

“It’s not a sport, it’s history.”

Chapter 41

Jamar made sure I got out of the side door okay after stopping at the hospital emergency entrance. The doors whooshed apart, and I followed the crew inside.

Drake's eyes blinked open and he struggled up on his elbows. "Amie."

Drake rolled off the bed and grimaced. Jamar caught him before he went all of the way to the floor. He pushed Drake back toward the bed. Drake resisted, balling his hand into a fist.

"It's okay, Drake." I stood behind Jamar. "I'm here. We're at the hospital. Relax."

Jamar and a couple of others eased him back onto the gurney. I followed them down the hall. They wheeled him into an exam room. I hesitated at the sliding glass door.

Jamar stopped next to me. "Thanks for the assist."

"We're not that close," I whispered, looking up at Jamar.

"Tonight, you are." Jamar nodded at me. My face heated up. Would we stay this close?

We watched them move Drake over to the emergency room bed. They strung the IVs around and hooked him up to the hospital's oxygen.

"Y'all have been through a lot. Why don't you stay here 'til y'alls parents arrive?" The nurse affirmed her agreement to what Jamar said. He bumped my shoulder when he left with the others.

My feet rooted themselves just outside the door. Blood taken, heart monitor hooked up, and a tech arrived to pull Drake out for x-rays. Drake gripped my hand on the way by.

Tressa ran up and attached herself to me, her eyes red and puffy. J-O-S-H SHOT. She buried her head into my shoulder and bawled.

Josh came by resting on his side. Blood-soaked gauze covered his hip and on his arm. My jaw dropped.

"It's not as bad as it looks." Josh winced.

"You got shot. How's that not serious?" My voice pitched louder.

"Two flesh wounds. No problem. You shoulda seen the blood the time I nailed myself in the calf with the staple gun." Josh shrugged. "Now that hurt."

He disappeared around the corner. Tressa followed my gaze. NO PROBLEM, HE SAYS.

WHAT? Tressa blinked tears away.

BOYS, I rolled my eyes.

A tiny smile lifted at the corners of her mouth. We stood there hugging.

Tressa's foster mom came around the corner soon afterwards. She signed to Tressa in warp deaf speed. There was no way for me to keep up with either of them. Josh's parents trailed after a nurse. His mom's knuckles white from squeezing her husband's hand. His fingers tinted purple, but he didn't seem to notice.

I expected Drake's parents to come around next. The hallway remained empty. My shoulders slumped. Where were they? I only saw them once or twice, but to be this late . . . why?

Footsteps ricocheted down the linoleum hallway. They did make it, after all.

Dad rounded the hall, his fire-line scowl firmly in place. No one messed with him then.

"Dad? When did you get back?" I launched myself into his embrace. My feet lifted off the floor in one of his bear hugs. They sometimes embarrassed me, but not this time. Tears snuck out. Did they never end?

"I've got you, Princess," He whispered in my ear. "You don't have to be tough right now."

Someone cleared their throat, "Excuse me, sir."

Dad set me down, tucking me under his shoulder. My hands wrapped around his sturdy waist.

“Logan Reid,” Dad exclaimed and held out his other hand. “Hey, man. I haven’t seen you since that fire out on the hill.”

Of course, my parents know everyone. Why did I assume they didn’t?

“Been awhile.” Deputy Logan stepped back, grinning. “I didn’t know Amie belonged to you. No wonder she gets into trouble.”

They both laughed.

“Thanks a lot,” I growled. My face boiled. Both men roared. The nursing staff scowled.

“I know who to call next time you end up on my radar.” Deputy Logan put his hands on his hips, his service weapon absent from its holster. He shifted, revealing another deputy with her blond hair in a braid, who stopped next to him. He nodded toward her. “I asked if I could come down to make the hand off easier, before going down for my own grilling.”

A vision of Deputy Logan walking across a barbeque grill flickered in front of my vision.

“Not that kind of grilling.” Dad smiled down as if he knew what I was thinking. “He’s going on administrative leave pending the investigation of the shooting.”

“Oh.” Reflective blankets and flashing lights came to mind. I pressed harder into Dad’s side.

“This is Kasey Williams. She’s a victim’s advocate and will be conducting the interviews.” They spoke together in a hushed tone. Deputy Logan sighed and started toward the exit.

“Where’s Mom and Grandpa?” I glanced around.

“Getting the video feed from Grandpa’s truck cam. Why does . . .” He paused, “Never mind. We’ll sort this out eventually.”

“Deputy Logan?” I called to him. He moved slower than I’d ever seen. He swiveled my direction.

“Yes, Ma’am.” He’d turned ten years older.

“Ma’am?” My face twisted, but the smile he gave didn’t reach his eyes. “Why aren’t Drake’s parents here?”

He glanced at Dad, who sighed and wagged his head. “They were the ones who attacked you at the cemetery.”

Chapter 42

Drake

The hospital room, his home for the next couple of days. Then what? The IV in his arm, no longer attached to the saline bag, itched. Free to pace the halls, but his body refused to allow much movement. Even breathing hurt. His stomach knotted. Would he have friends after this?

Amie walked into the room. Drake's neck heated up. Feeling underdressed, he pulled the blanket to his chest. The move sent a shimmer of pain down his side. A guy strode in behind her. He shared features with Amie. Or she with him? Except her dad, if that's who he was, had enough brawn to bench press him through the window.

Drake's mouth went dry. He sucked water out of his hospital cup, never taking his eyes off the man. Amie, more relaxed than he'd ever seen her, let her shoes fall to the floor as she tucked her legs under her in the reclining chair off to his right. She sported a cut on her lip. At least he saved her from the worst of the beating.

Mr. Muscle perched on the arm of the couch in his room. The nurse told him the couch folded out to a bed for family, but it'd remain empty.

"This is my dad," Amie beamed.

"Drake," Amie's dad stood and closed the distance, holding out his hand. Drake jerked back. "I'll be forever grateful for you saving my little girl's life."

Drake stared at the man's outstretched hand. His throat constricted, "I'm the traitor. I put her in danger."

The man's hand didn't budge. "Was it you or your parents?"

"I don't know," Drake's voice gave out. Admitting things to the police was one thing. Confessing to a dad? So much scarier. "It's what they trained me to do."

Drake's orders were to infiltrate. He did. His rib cage cramped up. Drake winced and rubbed the spasming muscle.

"My guess is you didn't get all of these," Amie's dad pointed to the bruises he saw, "breaking into my house."

Drake's left eye remained swollen shut. Breathing through his nose proved futile, and his shoulder ached like a jackhammer had gone through it. The doctor told him his bruised ribs weren't broken, but every time he inhaled, he gulped fire. To top it all off, the skin of his knuckles hurt from scraping headstones. At least the bottoms of his feet didn't hurt.

"Son, look at me." Drake winced. He swallowed hard and pushed his eyes up. Concern creased Amie's dad's brow. No anger. Drake tilted his head to the side. Curious.

"You'll always have a place at my table," Dad's voice wavered. Is that what pride sounded like? The meaty paw re-extended. Drake reached out and shook the proffered hand, the strong grip gentle.

"Thank you, sir." Drake ducked his head.

Josh limped in with his mom right behind him. She held Josh's elbow and eased him down to the couch.

"What happened to you?" Drake saw a bulge in Josh's shirt from a bandage.

"Your dad, I didn't know that then, shot me in the butt. Thankfully the second shot missed my head and grazed my arm."

Drake winced and snorted. He squeezed his knees to hold off the pain. "Sorry."

"I'm not. I whacked him twice. Once with a bat and the other with a baseball."

Drake gave Josh a thumbs up. Was it wrong to feel relief about being free from his parents?

Tressa stomped in and put a hand on her hip. She huffed, WE LOST. She rolled her eyes and flung her hands in the air.

NICE ENTRANCE. Drake signed.

Tressa curtsied. YOUR DAD SQUASHED OUR PROJECT. I MADE FAST ONE. USED LAMPSHADE. PRINT. CUT. HURRY, HURRY. NO NEXT ROUND. ALL THAT HARD WORK. She made a poof gesture and sighed. WE BETTER HAVE GOOD GRADE.

Tressa flopped on the couch next to Josh. He let out a silent scream. SORRY, she added. FORGOT BUTT HURT.

THANKS T-R-E-S-S-A FOR TRYING. Drake's hands ached from signing.

Tressa waved it off. She started to check on Josh and hesitated, rotating back to him. YOU SIGN! She clapped her hands and leaped to the side of the bed, cutting off his view of Amie.

TRY, Drake rubbed his hand. NO SCHOOL, HAD TIME LEARN.

GOOD JOB. She cocked her head to the side and squinted. YOU S-P-Y. WHAT SEARCHING FOR?

PAPERS FROM LONG AGO.

THIS? Tressa pulled out her phone and shoved it toward Drake's nose. He leaned away. The picture showed papers strewn all over the floor. He zoomed it in. The familiar Russian print easy to recognize.

YES.

Tressa swiped it to the next scene and displayed a young, beautiful woman. Softer eyes than his mother.

MY GRANDMOTHER, Drake answered her.

COOL.

WHERE YOU FIND? Drake cringed when he shrugged.

IN METAL BOX HIT YOUR MOM HEAD. POLICE TAKE.

GOOD. Drake nodded. Weariness ate at the edges of his energy. Too much to think about. Maybe Tressa's mom would keep him for a little while? Was he brave enough to ask?

Tressa tapped Drake's foot, he refocused on her. She returned to the frame with the papers. WHAT SAY?

Drake extended his trembling hand. Reading the missives proved tricky with one eye, even zooming in. "It's about a trip with a group of international students. She passed herself off as one." Drake stopped reading. "I can't translate more than one language at a time."

Tressa's mom glided to the other side of the hospital bed. Drake snapped his feet away, his knees thumped into his chest. He moaned.

"Sorry, Drake." Her foster mom stepped to the side. "How far back do I need to go for you to feel safe?"

She knew and it didn't bother her. "No. You're fine there."

Tressa's foster mom caught her up on what she missed.

MORE. Tressa rotated a wrist, wanting him to give her more.

Drake squinted at the screen again, "She kept track of everything. Her ultimate goal was to find a way to steal the uranium ore or set an explosion. She left the information with Pags and he buried it for a different spy to pick it up. That's all I can make out without seeing the actual documents themselves. I guess it's a good thing the uranium boom died from over supply when it did. My parents were tasked with retrieving all of the documents my grandma wrote on her tour. This set was the last state on our list."

"From the stories I've heard, I can see Pags doing that," Amie's dad shook his head.

"It explains the two graves," Josh shifted to the healthy hip.

"Speaking of documents," Deputy Will came to a halt inside the door. "I have a certificate and some test results I need to discuss."

"The letter," Amie exclaimed. "I forgot all about it. How'd the test come back so fast, doesn't it take weeks?"

"They allowed a rush on it." Deputy Will focused on Josh's Mom. "Mrs. Zovko, can you explain why Josh's DNA but not his fingerprints are on this letter?"

"What letter?" She glanced at Josh.

"What'd you do to get into the system?" Amie smirked.

Josh's neck turned red. "I may have gone missing for three days trying to walk to Australia."

OCEAN YOU THINK? Tressa made a fish face at him.

"I was four." Josh lifted a shoulder. "I never thought that far ahead. It would've been more fun if my carbon copy was with me. We'd have shared the punishment."

CARBON COPY? Tressa frowned.

Josh's eyes widened. Drake knew, deep down, because he forgot to sign. TWIN, Josh answered.

OH, I SEE. Tressa made a Y with her hand and dropped it like a yes.

Deputy Will showed Josh's mom the page. "That's not Josh's handwriting."

Josh leaned in, "That's Drake's."

Everyone turned their attention on him. Drake's heart cranked up. "I . . . I . . .wanted to keep Amie safe. Pushing her away seemed the best way to keep her out of the fallout of my life. It didn't work." Drake grimaced at Amie's dad. "Sorry about the burner phone."

"We had a long talk about it." Amie drew an L slowly up her arm. "Really, really long talk."

Her dad smiled. Josh's mom had a weird look on her face.

Drake frowned at Deputy Will, "What about the certificate?"

"The FBI found your birth certificate, Drake, and confirmed it was a forgery when they searched the home." Deputy Will opened his mouth to say more.

Amie beat him to it, "The FBI?"

"Yep. Drake's parents, um, kidnappers are on the most wanted list for espionage and other fraud charges."

The espionage he lived through, but kidnapping? He cocked his head to the side. "They're the only parents I remember, they didn't steal me."

"Well, that wasn't everyone's first assumption either, however, they dug around in the hospital records and mothballed case files. They discovered a stolen baby for that date." Deputy Will adjusted his vest. "No one remembers anything when they're two days old."

Josh's mom gasped. Tears streamed down her cheeks. "Drake? Your name is Drake?"

Worry etched Josh's face. "I mentioned him before."

"Yes, ma'am." Drake fisted the bed sheets.

Her hand covered her mouth. "My son?"

"Mom, my twin was named Christopher."

"Christopher Drake," she whispered.

"I'm Drake Christopher." His skin crawled. What did this mean for him? Nothing made sense. His head buzzed. No way this was true. Right?

Drake looked at Amie. Her face morphed from shock to a smile. COOL. She signed to him.

Josh's mom stood, not taking her eyes off him. "What do I have to do to reclaim my son?"

He had a different mom. Moments before his freedom spelled possibilities. Now prison bars confined his thinking. How would she treat him? A headache sprouted at the base of his skull.

"Shouldn't be much." Deputy Will shook his head and continued, "You still have Drake's birth certificate with his feet and handprints?"

"Absolutely," she drifted closer to Drake.

"The FBI or our techs will need to see it to confirm." Deputy Will scratched his head.

Drake shrank back and cringed. How angry did she get?

Josh's mom stopped at his bedside. "Can I sit on the bed next to you?"

"Uh." Drake leaned back to see Amie.

"She's nice. She leaves the room when she gets upset. That's what she did when we tracked mud through the house when they helped with Grandpa's truck last summer." Amie read his thoughts. It was nice being close to someone for a change.

Josh agreed with a dip of his head.

"Okay," Drake croaked and closed his good eye.

The bed shifted where she sat. After a long moment, he peeked. Josh's mom lifted her hand. Drake instinctively lurched back. Pain erupted through his torso. He cried out.

"I'm sorry," fresh tears spilled from her eyes.

Tears? Sorry? Mom never did that. Frowning, he reached his left hand out and captured a tear from her chin.

"Why are you sorry?" Drake watched the water droplet fall on the blanket.

"Honey, I've missed you. There's a you-shaped hole in my heart. It's been there for sixteen years, two months, and eleven days. And now, when I do find you," she stifled a sob. "Someone's turned you into a punching bag."

"You counted?" Drake and Josh said together.

"Yes," she laughed, moving forward, she stopped, and brought her hands back under her chin.

WHY WE NOT SEE BEFORE? Tressa held her hands out.

WE DID. SMALL. Amie paused. NOT ENOUGH PUZZLE PIECES.

THAT! Tressa pointed at Amie.

"What did you want to do just now?" Drake's shoulders sagged. The adrenaline rollercoaster and need to protect himself, left him edgy and tired.

"Hug you and not let go," she sniffled.

"Hug?" Drake moved his head to the side.

Tressa pointed at Drake with two fingers and moved them back to herself. WATCH ME. She marched over to Amie and put her arms around her. Tressa turned. SAME.

"She never hugged you?" Mom made a funny hiccup sound.

"No." He ducked his chin. How much did he miss? "I never gave her a reason to."

A low growl came from both men. Deputy Will and Amie's dad's faces became unreadable.

"Excuse us," Dad rasped. They exited the room.

"It's okay." Amie signed, CALM DOWN. "Let them be angry for you."

"For me? What's that mean?" Drake replied.

"It means they don't like the injustice of it all. Hugs aren't something you earn. They're what you give away because you can. You may have a few more guys hanging out with you and your dad soon doing mentoring stuff, like teaching you self-defense, camping."

"Let's do it," Josh pumped a fist. Drake nodded.

His mom readjusted to sit hip to hip, facing him. She touched both of his shoulders and drew him forward. His good cheek rested on her shoulder. It was soft. Mom hummed a song he'd never heard before. Amie hummed along.

This mom, his mom, was safe.

Warmth filled his chest. Drake closed his eyes and allowed sleep to claim him.

Chapter 43

Five Months Later: Amie

SPARKLE. Tressa bounced along the bleacher seat and plopped next to me. Yep, the name sign stuck. I had time to talk her out of it when we went to her church camp this summer. URANIUM DOWNS. I LIKE BMX MORE. NO DOG RACE. BOYS CUTER.

Drake, Josh, Tressa and I had taken to calling the fairgrounds by its original name. Since Monica and Mona knew too, it became our inside joke.

I rolled my eyes and kept on knitting, the bamboo needles flying in my hands. I had six months of knitting to catch up on. My crimes had piled high. Tressa and I texted in a constant stream when we weren't together.

Grandpa, Mom, Dad, and I all arrived early and settled in. A fire broke out along the interstate near the Colorado-Utah border that they had to leave for. They dropped

Grandpa off at the house first so he could bring back his truck. The start of fire season.

Monica and Pierce Estes strolled up. She wore a t-shirt with plaid pants and skater shoes. Monica's family agreed to take Pierce in after finding out his mom beat him. Pierce mellowed out and wasn't such a weird jerk now that he spoke with a counselor. He dyed his hair all one color and wore all black. He'd made peace with Tressa, although she still called him Skunk. Drake didn't even mind. Monica and Pierce sat one row in front of us. Pierce leaned their skateboards on the seat next to him. Pierce told me he didn't like BMX and quit competing in it after the race in December.

Jamar and Mona Billings settled to my right.

"Hope you don't mind me being here." Jamar waved at Tressa. "I had a day off. And I needed to tell you something, Amie."

"The more the merrier." I grinned.

WHY TOGETHER? Tressa jabbed my arm.

I pointed to Jamar and Mona. COUSINS.

COOL. Tressa waved back.

"Tell me what?" I watched Jamar's face turn serious.

"I told you Drake wouldn't die." He winked at me.

I smiled.

"Jamar," Josh's mom had to shout around her gaggle of girls clanking along the bleachers. Josh's dad carried their bleacher seats. "School lets out next week. We're celebrating with a barbeque. You should come if you aren't at the firehouse. Or come with the others from the firehouse." Drake and Josh's parents made a point to see a counselor every week after Drake moved in. Dad kept Deputy Will and Deputy Logan updated on his progress. The three of them planned a camping trip in the near future with the Zovko men. The ladies all planned on going hiking or the spa, or both.

"Thank you, I'll let the shift know and see what they say." Jamar called back. "Amie, your grandpa looks like he needs rescuin'."

"Yoohoo," the older lady who flirted with Grandpa back in December waved. Her grandson always lined up next to Drake for the same conversation before each race. We all dubbed him Sir Talks-a-Lot. His grandma told me once that Grandpa was as handsome as Thor. I failed to see the resemblance.

Grandpa walked faster than I ever saw him move before. Determination propelled him forward. He called out, "Pierce, move the skateboard and sit down a row. Sir Talks-a-Lot's grandmother is trying to get me to take her out on a date."

Pierce squared his shoulders and lifted his chin. He slid over and down a row.

Grandpa landed with a huff, "Thank you, Son." He patted Pierce's back.

Pierce rotated to check on him, "Anything for you, Grandpa."

Mona moved down to sit next to Grandpa and hugged his arm.

"Thanks, Darlin'." He sighed. "Jamar, is that you back there?"

"It is," Jamar answered.

"I hear you received a commendation the other day. Your grandfather would be proud of you."

"Thanks, Grandpa. We got your back too." Jamar bumped my elbow and moved his chin toward the lady. She stomped her foot and chose to sit on the other side of Drake and Josh's family. Jamar laughed. We bumped fists.

Drake and Josh's youngest twin sisters came up and leaned on Tressa's knees. They had a twinkle of challenge in their eyes. NO ONE LOUDER US.

They had the same conversation before every race. It usually ended in an argument. Today, a crooked smile shifted Tressa's face. Mischief lit her eyes. I plugged my ears. She lifted her hand and gave a short blast of an air horn in their faces.

YOU WIN. AGAIN. They tromped off.

Tressa wagged her eyebrows at me.

DON'T MAKE THEM DEAF. I signed.

STOPPED ARGUMENT. NEXT TIME ONLY NEED SHOW. She held up the air horn.

Mona explained to Jamar what happened between Tressa and twins and why, and he slapped his knee and gave Tressa a thumbs up.

Everyone knew Tressa's air horn. She found a way for Josh to hear her out on the track.

Josh embraced BMX as a sport. The twins found a way to practice before they opened back up. He'd caught up to Drake's skill level in no time. They talked about finding a coach together. On the flipside, Drake's driving test happened sometime next week. He and Josh planned on sharing the Jeep for now.

Today's race prepared them to race at state or nationals. I think. Maybe. I wouldn't tell Drake I forgot. He'd say I'd need to write it in yarn to remember.

Checking a stitch, I scowled at Tressa when she punched my arm. She ignored me and pointed to the starting line. Josh and Drake waved. Our whole group waved back.

Knitting in my lap, I waited for the race to start. Both boys launched down the track, hitting turns and pumping hard.

Drake rose above Josh at a turn and then cut low, gaining the advantage. Drake ended up edging out Josh by a tire tread. I'd miss them when they went on the road this summer for competition. They even talked about races around the country next school year.

"Hey, since you're into local history," Jamar called our attention. "Did ya hear about how they think they smuggled rum out from under the train depot during Prohibition?"

THE END

Acknowledgments

Even though I write alone, I'm never alone. God's given me an amazing gift for words to share with others. Plus, there's a whole crew backing me up along this whole journey. My family has been great in the advice department, support they've offered, and helping to fact check my work. A big thank you to Andrew Callor and my other BMX cousins for answering questions and posting races and trainings, any mistakes are completely mine, not theirs. The special collections and reference librarians at Colorado Mesa University, thanks for helping me sort out the research for this project. Many thanks my law enforcement friends for telling me countless stories and to Chris, who made sure I got my information right – any extra goofs are my own. To Staci Nichols for helping me understand deaf culture and helped me turn Tressa into a cool character. Thanks Debra S. and Olivia Hebrank for catching my editing issues. Marc Melnick, the cover photos turned out great! Thank you so much, this is the icing on the cake. What would I do without my brainstorm crew and my beta readers? You rock! Thank you to my Word Weavers group and my writer tribe, you helped me see the trees in the forest. Many thanks to the Rubart Writing Academy for giving me that extra push in knowing my strengths. Broken Yoke Publications: thanks for believing in me and taking a chance with this book and collection!

Thanks for diving into this story with me. If you like it, could you leave me a review?

BROKEN YOKE

PUBLISHING

brokenyokepublishing.com